Dear Reader,

We are deeply saddened to have to say goodbye to Betty Neels, who was one of our best-loved authors, as well as being a wonderfully warm and thoroughly charming woman. She led a fascinating life even before becoming a writer, and her publishing record was impressive.

Over her thirty-year career, Betty wrote more than 134 novels, and published in more than one hundred international markets. She continued to write into her ninetieth year, remaining as passionate about her characters and stories then as she was in her very first book. Betty Neels was prolific, and we have a number of new titles to feature in our forthcoming publishing programs.

Betty will be greatly missed, both by her friends within Harlequin and by her legions of loyal readers around the world. Our deepest sympathy and condolences are with her family at this time.

Yours sincerely,

Harlequin Books

Betty Neels spent her childhood and youth in Devonshire before training as a nurse and midwife. She was an army nursing sister during the war, married a Dutchman and subsequently lived in Holland for fourteen years. Betty started to write on retirement from nursing, incited by a lady in a library bemoaning the lack of romance novels. She has become a prolific and well-loved author.

THE BEST *of*
BETTY NEELS
VISITING CONSULTANT

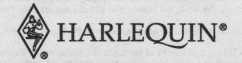

HARLEQUIN®

TORONTO • NEW YORK • LONDON
AMSTERDAM • PARIS • SYDNEY • HAMBURG
STOCKHOLM • ATHENS • TOKYO • MILAN • MADRID
PRAGUE • WARSAW • BUDAPEST • AUCKLAND

ISBN 0-373-51165-5

VISITING CONSULTANT

First North American Publication 2001

Copyright © 1969 by Betty Neels.

This edition published by arrangement with Harlequin Books S.A.

® and TM are trademarks of the publisher. Trademarks indicated with ® are registered in the United States Patent and Trademark Office, the Canadian Trade Marks Office and in other countries.

Visit us at www.eHarlequin.com

Printed in U.S.A.

CHAPTER ONE

SISTER SOPHIA Greenslade wrinkled her straight little nose under her muslin mask and thought longingly of her tea. The theatre list should have been finished an hour ago, but an emergency splenectomy had had to be fitted in during the afternoon. Now the last case, a simple appendicectomy, was on the table. The RSO, Tom Carruthers, put out a gloved hand to take the purse string she had ready. She fitted a curved, threaded needle into its holder, and glanced at the clock. Five minutes, she calculated, and she'd be free. Staff had been back on duty for more than half an hour; she could hand over to her. She passed the stitch scissors at exactly the right moment; nodded to the junior nurse to check swabs, and started to put the soiled instruments into the bowl of saline nearby, pausing only to put a threaded skin needle into the mute demanding hand of the RSO. Raising a pair of nicely-shaped eyebrows at a watching nurse, who had been long enough in theatre to know what the gesture signified—to whisk the bowl away—Sister Greenslade got down from the small square stool behind her white-draped trolleys and stationed herself by the houseman opposite Tom Carruthers, ready to clap on the small piece of strapping over the neatly stitched wound. This done to her satisfaction, she said 'Porters, please' in her nice, unhurried voice, and followed the RSO over to the sink, stooping to pick up his gown and cap which he had shed as he went. Inured to the ways of surgeons, she said nothing, but put them wordlessly into the bin and stood quietly while a nurse untied the tapes of her own gown, then took off her theatre cap and mask, revealing a pleasant face, redeemed from plainness by a pair of magnificent eyes with very dark lashes. Her nose was nondescript, and her mouth too large; her complexion was good, and her hair, drawn severely back into a coil on top of her head, was a delicate shade of mouse. She was barely middle height, but her figure, which was charming, more than compensated for her lack of inches.

She joined the two men at the sinks in the scrubbing room, and they stood in a row, relaxed and friendly, all of them anxious to be gone.

'What's the time?' asked Tom.

Sophia went on scrubbing. 'Almost six,' she said. 'If you hurry and your wife's waiting and ready, you'll just about get there as the curtain goes up.'

She smiled up at him, and he thought for the hundredth time that her smile transformed her whole face. He was a happily married man himself, he couldn't understand why Sister Greenslade hadn't been snapped up before now. He started to dry his hands.

'What about you? Got a date to-night?'

She turned off the taps and said with a twinkle, 'They're falling over themselves to get at me—it's my fatal beauty.' She chuckled at her own remark, and went away to hand over.

Ten minutes later, she was on her way home. The early October evening was already chilly, but after the warmth of the theatre she welcomed its freshness.

The hospital was in a pleasant part of London; the houses around it were for the most part elderly and terraced and well cared-for. There were lighted windows in most of them as she hurried towards her own home. She had been a very small girl when her father, a consultant at the hospital, had bought it. When he and her mother had been killed in a road accident, she had been just twenty-one, newly registered, and staffing in theatre. Her parents' death had been a sorrow she had been forced to bury deep under the responsibilities she had shouldered. The three younger children had still been at school then, and somehow she had been able to keep the home together, dividing her busy life between the exacting roles of mother, housekeeper and nurse with a success which had been earned at the expense of a much curtailed social life. In this she had been greatly helped by Grandmother Greenslade, who lived with them, and Sinclair, who had been her father's batman in the army during the war, and had somehow attached himself to his household when they had been demobbed. Indeed, he was the staunch friend of the whole family, and stood high in their affections.

She turned the last corner into the street where she lived. The house was half way down; she could see it quite clearly, even in the dusk. She could also see a small boy standing on the pavement—her younger brother, Benjamin. She frowned, and walked faster. Ben had a habit of getting into scrapes, which was probably why the tall gentleman with him was holding him so firmly by one shoulder. As she reached them, her mouth was open to utter some soothing phrase. She was forestalled, however.

'Ah, Sister Sophy, I fancy.' The voice sounded impatient and faintly mocking. She took a look at the speaker; he was not only tall, but big, with an air of self-confidence, almost arrogance, which made his good-looking face seem older than it probably was. He returned her look with the coldest blue eyes she had seen for a very long time.

Sophy listened to the sudden thump of her heart. She was, she told herself, very angry.

'Yes, my name is Sophy,' she said coolly. 'Though I can't imagine why you should be so ill-mannered and—and familiar.'

He put his handsome head a little on one side—the street lamp's thin light turned his grey hair to silver—and said silkily, to madden her,

'My dear good madam, why should I wish to be familiar with you? I used your name merely as a means of identification.'

Sophy choked, drew a long calming breath, and turned to her brother.

'What have you done, Ben?' she asked resignedly. Then, as she saw his white face, 'Are you hurt? What happened?'

Ben looked at her with relief mingled with a twelve-year-old boy's revulsion of making a scene.

'I bumped into this gentleman's car...'

The gentleman interrupted crisply,

'You should teach your brother that it's unwise to run across a street before looking to see if it's empty.'

It was at this moment that Sophy became aware of the gleaming Bentley drawn up at the kerb. She thought it unlikely that it had been damaged, it appeared to be perfection itself.

'I expect you were driving too fast,' she said outrageously.

He laughed with real amusement.

'I think not,' he said, the laugh echoing in his voice. 'I'm not in the habit of driving recklessly; and may I remind you that it's I who have the right to be annoyed, not you? I dislike being forced to avoid small boys and large dogs—'

Sophy stared at him, and repeated 'Large dogs?' in a rather thin voice, and then—'The Blot!' in a tone of consternation. She whipped off a glove, put two fingers into her mouth and whistled piercingly, causing her two companions to wince, then turned to her brother.

'Ben, I told you not to let the Blot cross the road without his lead!'

'I didn't, truly, Sophy. But Titus went with us and sat down in the park and wouldn't come back; so of course the moment I took the Blot's lead off, he went back for him.' He paused. 'I had to go after him, didn't I?'

Sophy considered the point gravely, her eyes on the stranger's well-cut tweed jacket. 'Yes,' she conceded, 'I suppose you did.'

She stopped talking to watch a large black dog, who from his appearance had been richly endowed by a large variety of unknown ancestors. The dog crossed the road with all the care of a child who has recently learned his kerb drill; his liquid black eye fixed on the man, as if to challenge him to think otherwise. The dog was closely followed by a nondescript cat, whose obvious low breeding was offset by a tremendous dignity.

Sophy heaved a sigh of relief. 'There they are,' she cried unnecessarily. 'They're devoted to each other,' she added, as an afterthought and in a tone of finality, as though that fact could explain away the whole episode. She heaved a sigh of relief which turned to a gasp. 'They didn't damage your car, did they?'

She looked up at the silent man beside her, and tried not to see how very handsome he was. The Blot had reared himself on to his hind legs, intent on making friends. The man patted him absent-mindedly, and looked down with resignation at Titus, who had wreathed himself around one elegant trousered leg. He shifted his gaze to Sophy, and said, 'Bentleys don't—er—dent very easily.'

'I say, is she really yours, sir?' Ben's enthusiasm had overcome his fright.

The black eyebrows rose. 'Most certainly.'

The boy looked at the graceful sweep of the car's bonnet.

'Well, I'd rather be run down by a Bentley than anything else,' he stated. 'Excepting a Rolls-Royce, of course.'

'If I only I'd known,' murmured the tall man, 'I would have done my best to oblige you.'

Sophy, deprived of her tea, and anxious to be gone from this strangely disturbing man, said sharply, 'What a great pity it is that you aren't driving your Rolls today.' And then stood abashed at his grave agreement and casual explanation that he seldom brought it to England. 'The Bentley is usually sufficient for my needs,' he concluded gently.

Sophy felt the colour surge into her face, and was thankful for the gathering darkness. She said in a stiff voice, 'I beg your pardon. If you're sure that Ben has done no harm, we'll go... Ben, will you apologise for upsetting this gentleman?'

'Do I look upset?' He was smiling openly at her, and her cheeks caught fire anew. He listened to Ben's apology and then put out a hand and tweaked the boy's ear gently. 'Goodbye,' he said, and turned away to his car, then, his hand on the door, looked over his shoulder.

'Blot,' he said. 'Escutcheon or Landscape?'

'Landscape,' said Sophy. 'We haven't got an escutcheon.'

'And Titus? One feels that it should have some Latin significance...but I'm at a loss.'

'He likes porridge.'

His shoulders shook. 'How slow-witted I've become; or perhaps my knowledge of your history is becoming a little rusty.' He got into the car. Above the restrained purr of the engine they heard his voice wishing them a goodnight.

Sophy closed the door behind her small party, took off her coat in the hall, warned Ben to wash his hands, and went straight to the kitchen. Sinclair glanced up as she went in, and then went on pouring water into a comfortably sized tea pot.

'You're very late, Miss Sophy. Thought I heard you talking outside in the street,' he went on innocently. The kitchen was at the back of the house, a point Sophy knew was not worth the mentioning.

'Ben ran in front of a car—we stopped to apologise to the driver.'

'Annoyed, was he? Ought to know better, these fast drivers; running innocent children down...'

Sophy perched on the edge of the kitchen table.

'Oh, Sinclair, it wasn't like that at all. It was Ben's fault, and this man was…very nice,' she ended tamely. Nice wasn't at all the right word… She thought of a great many adjectives which would describe him. He had annoyed her, and mocked her, and made her feel silly, as though she had been a brash teenager; but she knew, without having to think about it, that if Ben had been knocked down he was the man she would have wished to be first on the scene.

She asked on a sigh, 'What's for supper, Sinclair? I missed tea.'

'Your grandma said a nice cauliflower cheese, miss. You go and have a cuppa, and I'll get it on the go for you.'

The three occupants of the sitting room all looked up as Sophy entered. And they all spoke simultaneously.

'Sophy, what is all this about a man and a car?

'He wasn't English, was he, Sophy? Even though he did understand about Titus… He said he had a Rolls, didn't he? Penny says I'm fibbing.'

'He looked gorgeous!' This from her sister, Penelope, in the tones of a love-sick tragedy queen.

Sophy put down the tea tray, poured herself a cup, and answered the questions without hurry or visible excitement. She smiled across the room at her grandmother, sitting comfortably by the fire, solving the *Telegraph* crossword in a leisurely fashion.

'Ben was almost knocked down by a car—it was his fault. We stopped to apologise to the driver. He was very nice about it.'

Her grandmother looked up, her pretty, absurdly

youthful face full of interest. 'Well, well. A man? Very good-looking, Penny says.'

Sophy replied composedly, 'Yes, very. And I think Benjamin's right in supposing him to be a foreigner.'

Penelope sighed gustily. At fifteen, she was full of romantic notions which at times made her very difficult to live with.

'He was a smasher. I couldn't see him quite clearly from the window. You might have asked him in, Sophy. Why didn't you?'

Sophy looked surprised. 'I didn't think about it,' she replied honestly, and then took pity on the pretty downcast face of her young sister. 'He wasn't very young,' she ventured.

'I'm old for my years,' Penny insisted. 'Age doesn't matter where true love exists.'

This profound remark drew forth general laughter in which Penny quite cheerfully joined, and then she said, 'Well, perhaps he was a bit old for me, but he would have done nicely for you, Sophy. You always said that you wished a tall handsome man would load you with jewels and furs and carry you off to his castle.'

Sophy looked astonished. 'Did I really say that?' Half-forgotten dreams, smothered by the prosaic daily round of her busy life, made her heart stir. She shook her head and said briskly. 'That must have been years ago.'

She was almost asleep in a sleeping house, when she remembered that he had said goodnight and not goodbye. She told herself sleepily that it meant nothing at all; but it was comforting all the same.

The tide of early morning chores washed away all

but the most commonplace of her thoughts. Even on
her short walk to the hospital her thoughts were taken
up with her elder brother, Luke, who was in his last
year of medical school at Edinburgh Royal. He was
twenty-two, almost four years younger than she; and
clever. What money there was she used ungrudgingly
to get him through his studies. Another year, and he
would qualify, and the money could be used for
Penny, and later, for Benjamin. The darkling thought
that by then she would be in her forties dimmed her
plans momentarily, but she wasn't a girl to give way
to self-pity, and she was cheerful enough as she went
along to the scrubbing room, and then into the theatre.
Staff Nurse had already laid up—the theatre was
ready.

Sophy began to thread her needles. She could hear
the murmur of men's voices in the scrubbing room.
The first case was to be a tricky one—a duodenopan-
createctomy—and Mr Giles Radcliffe, the senior consultant surgeon, would be doing it. Probably the RSO
would assist, for Mr Radcliffe's houseman was fresh
from his training school, and though painfully anxious
to please, still leaned heavily on Sophy's unobtrusive
help, given wordlessly by means of frowns and nods
and seeing that the correct instrument was always
ready to his hand. She looked up as they came in,
and her 'Good morning' froze on her lips. There were
three men, not two. The third one was the man with
the Bentley. Even gowned and masked, it was impossible not to recognise those pale blue eyes. They
were staring at her now, with an expression which
she was unable to read.

CHAPTER TWO

THE THREE SURGEONS strolled across the theatre with an air of not having much to do. Mr Radcliffe glanced at the patient before he spoke.

'Sophy, this is Professor Jonkheer Maximillan van Oosterwelde—he will be operating this morning.'

He turned to the tall man with him. 'Max, this is Miss Sophia Greenslade, Sister in charge of Main Theatre.'

They looked at each other over their masks—Sophy's lovely hazel eyes, wide with surprise, encountered his cool blue ones. She said something—she had no idea what—in a murmur. Jonkheer van Oosterwelde said 'How do you do?' in a voice which really didn't want to know, and turned to his patient.

Sophy had no time to wonder why her heart was racing and her cheeks were burning. Training and discipline clamped down on her muddled thoughts; she passed Bill Evans the sponges for the final prep, and handed Mr Radcliffe a large sterile sheet, which the surgeons arranged with all the meticulous care of housewives draping the best tablecloth. It shrouded the quiet figure between them in decent obscurity; leaving a surprisingly small area of skin exposed. She followed it with a variety of small towels and towel clips, and waited composedly until the anaesthetist said 'Ready when you are.' And when a quiet voice said, 'Right, Sister,' she was ready with the knife, and

then in quick succession, the tissue and artery forceps
and swabs. Mr Radcliffe put out a hand for gut, and
she handed the retractors to Bill, then looked quickly
round the theatre. She had a good team of nurses; they
were all doing their allotted tasks. She nodded at each
in turn and raised her eyebrows at Staff, who slid up
behind her, whispered 'Sucker?' and switched it on.
Sophy passed its sterile nozzle to Bill, who was looking worried because he hadn't got anything to do. He
took it gratefully, feeling he was in the picture again.
She checked the clamps and the intestinal needles,
rinsed the discarded forceps and put them ready to
hand again, and watched Jonkheer van Oosterwelde.
He was looking ahead of him, probing with gentle
fingers; intent on his delicate task. At length he fo-
cused his gaze on Mr Radcliffe.

'It's worth trying, I think—what would you say?'

Sophy watched while Mr Radcliffe did exactly the
same thing in his turn, then nodded. She caught a
nurse's eye and looked silently at the bowls. The
nurse changed the saline in them and went away for
a fresh supply; the operation would be a long one.
The vacoliter would need changing fairly soon; she
lifted a gloved finger and the junior nurse slid away
to fetch a fresh supply. The men were talking quietly,
working in unison. The Dutchman was dissecting
with slow delicacy; Sophy put up a warning finger
again, and a nurse edged up to the table with a receiver, to receive the result of his painstaking work.
He stretched his long back, and bent to his work
again, and Mr Radcliffe said,

'You're too tall, Max, by at least six inches—a pity
you can't give some of them to Sophy. She has to

stand on a box—when you see her on the ground, you'll see what I mean.'

'I know perfectly what you mean; I have already seen her on the ground.' He took an atraumatic needle from Sophy without looking at her.

'You've met already? Where?'

'In the street, yesterday evening, but we—ah—didn't introduce ourselves.'

Sophy thought he was laughing behind his mask. She said tartly, 'Which number gut will you use, sir?'

He had started the long-drawn out business of implanting, and didn't look up from his work, but answered her in quite a different voice in which she could not detect the smallest thread of a laugh; and though the two men, and even Bill, talked among themselves during the remainder of the operation she was not included in their conversation. It wasn't until the patient had been borne carefully away and Mr Radcliffe had rather tiredly suggested that they have coffee before the next case, that the other man spoke.

'Thank you for your help, Sister—you are, if I may say so, very good at your job.'

Mr Radcliffe looked over his shoulder as he went through the door.

'Yes, of course she is. Sophy, come and have your coffee with us—I want to talk to you.'

There was nothing for it but to do as she was asked. The theatre was already cleared and with whispered instructions to Staff to scrub and lay up as soon as she had had her coffee, Sophy followed the three men into her office. They stood politely while she took the chair behind her desk and then settled themselves: Mr Radcliffe on to the only other chair the room contained, Bill Evans on the edge of the desk, the Dutch-man on the low window ledge. They were still wear-ing their caps and rubber boots and thick, enveloping aprons; the rubber smelled pungently in the small room. Tieless shirts and rolled-up sleeves did nothing to add to the general aspect of their appearance, but Sophy was used to it and indeed hardly noticed it as she poured coffee into the gaily painted mugs the nurses had given her for Christmas. She ladled in gen-erous spoonfuls of sugar, and handed round the heart-ening beverage, and offered digestive biscuits with an unselfconscious, almost motherly air. The talk was pure shop, and she joined in easily; accepted as some-one who knew what was being talked about and could be depended upon to listen with intelligence and give the right answers. Mr Radcliffe barely gave Bill time to drink his coffee before sending him off to the ward on an errand. As the door closed he passed his mug for a second cup and said,

'I'm going on holiday, Sophy—for about six weeks.'

Sophy blinked her amazingly long eyelashes and said nothing.

'I've been advised to rest for a bit, Max has kindly agreed to take over while I'm away, for the first few weeks at least. His own theatre in Utrecht is being rebuilt—it couldn't be more fortuitous.'

Sophy filled the Dutch surgeon's mug, and said quietly, 'You're ill, Uncle Giles, aren't you?'

She handed Professor Jonkheer van Oosterwelde his coffee, ignoring his raised eyebrows. He had hardly spoken a dozen words to her, and for all she cared, she thought defiantly, he need not bother to address her again. She turned back to the older man.

Mr Radcliffe was no fool. He had seen the raised brows and the heightened colour in Sophy's cheeks. He didn't answer her question, but said smoothly, 'Your fathers were my two greatest friends, although they never met. I stood godfather to each of you in turn, you know.' He coughed, 'Strange that you should meet like this.'

Max van Oosterwelde got up, apparently unaware of Sophy's interested stare. 'Very strange,' he agreed dryly. 'I imagine there was a decade or so between your good offices, however.'

'But that doesn't matter,' cried Sophy, 'It makes us into readymade...' She paused. She had been about to say friends, but they weren't friends, and the look she had just encountered held very little warmth in it, merely a faint, derisive amusement. She blushed, then frowned heavily, and was thankful when Uncle Giles got up too and remarked that it was time they got on with the job again.

They worked steadily for the next couple of hours. The nurses went in turn to their dinners, and when Sophy eventually went to her own, it was past two o'clock. She ate it, as she had so often done, in the complete silence of the empty dining room, thinking about the morning. She had exchanged barely a dozen words with the new surgeon after the coffee break. He was pleasant—and easy—to work for, she admitted to herself, but he obviously had no intention of being friendly. It was at this point that she realised that she knew nothing about him—perhaps he was married? or engaged? She felt unaccountably depressed at the thought; the not very appetising meal became uneatable, and she went back to the theatre.

The men came back from their own lunch in excellent spirits, and Jonkheer van Oosterwelde removed a gall bladder, repaired two tricky hernias, and whisked out a couple of appendices with a neatness and dispatch which could only earn Sophy's admiration; maintaining an easy flow of conversation while he did so, while rather markedly excluding her from it. Not that he was anything but polite and correct towards her; indeed, when she inadvertently dropped the stitch scissors she was made very aware of his patient tolerance towards her clumsiness.

The last case was wheeled out of the theatre just before five o'clock, and the three men, shedding gowns and caps as they went, followed it. Sophy and her nurses plunged into the business of clearing the theatre, and made such good work of it that after ten minutes Sophy felt justified in leaving Staff Nurse to do the knives and needles, and go off duty. She went down the passage to her office and went in. The little room was wreathed in tobacco smoke; she swallowed a sigh, as Uncle Giles caught her eye and asked, 'Tea, Sophy?'

She said quietly, 'Of course, it won't take a minute.'

She went back into the tiny kitchen where a kettle was kept perpetually on the boil and a tray stood ready, made the tea and carried it back and poured it out before turning to go. In this she was frustrated, however. The Dutchman was standing by the window, his broad shoulders blocking what light there was, his great height dwarfing everything else around him.

'You will have a cup, too, Sister?' There was no warmth in his voice. Sophy said baldly, 'No,' and then, because it had sounded rude, 'Thank you. I'm going off duty.'

He didn't answer, but bent forward and poured another cup of tea and handed it to her, so that she was forced to take it and sit in the chair he pulled out from behind her desk. He said gently, as though she hadn't spoken, 'It will only take a minute; it would be a pity to miss your tea.'

She looked at her cup, angry with herself for going red, and Mr Radcliffe, noticing her hot cheeks, put down his own cup and asked,

'How did you two meet?'

Sophy remained stubbornly silent, and after a minute Jonkheer van Oosterwelde gave him a brief account of their encounter. She sat listening to his deep voice making light of the whole affair and cheerfully taking the blame upon himself. She felt faintly ashamed of herself, then remembered how he had addressed her as his dear madam. Her cheeks grew fiery again at the recollection, their redness fanned by the amused stare she encountered when she ventured to glance at him.

Her godfather thought it was all rather amusing, and said so before launching into an anecdote of his own. Under cover of this, Bill bent forward.

'Sister Greenslade, you haven't forgotten I'm coming to supper on Saturday evening?' he asked eagerly. 'I mean, if it's still all right...'

Sophy smiled warmly at him. 'Of course it's all

right. Come early, then we can play Monopoly or Canasta after supper.'

She got up to go, and Mr Radcliffe paused in his low-voiced talk.

'Your aunt expects you all on Sunday, Sophy—she told me to remind you.'

She stood in the doorway, very neat in her blue dress. She had put her cap on when she had gone to make the tea; it perched, like an ultra-clean butterfly, on top of her tidy head. All three men were watching her, but she was looking at her godfather.

'Thank you, Uncle Giles. We love coming; you know that. We shall miss it while you're away.' She smiled, murmured a pleasant 'Goodnight' and shut the door quietly behind her.

The theatre was clear; she sent the nurses off duty, had a word with Staff, and went to the changing room, from whence she emerged ten minutes later, still looking neat, in a nicely cut tweed suit; its rich greens and browns suited her—the man following her quietly away from the theatre block and down the staircase thought so too. Sophy hadn't heard him until his voice asked just behind her,

'Can I give you a lift?'

'No, thank you.' The words were spoken before she could regret them. It would be nice to ride in a Bentley. 'I live quite close.' And added crossly, 'You know that,' she paused, 'sir.'

'I'm afraid I made you late, suggesting that you should have tea just now. Allow me to make amends.'

He crossed the entrance hall with her, obviously sure of getting his own way. They said goodnight to Pratt, the head porter, and she went through the heavy door which he held open for her. She only had to say that she preferred to walk, but somehow the words wouldn't come. She found herself sitting beside him. The temptation to sink back into the rich cosiness of the leather was great; instead, she sat upright, looking ahead of her, as though she had never seen the streets before. He turned to look at her as they slid along the familiar route.

'You don't have to be on your guard all the time, do you?'

Sophy felt the soft hammer of her heart. 'I don't know what you mean,' she said, too quickly.

'Yes, you do, some time we'll discuss it, but to begin with you might try sitting back comfortably, even if it is only for a few minutes. I must say I'm surprised. I thought you were a sensible sort of young woman.'

Sophy felt rage wash over her—why did he contrive to make her feel foolish? 'I've no idea what you're talking about,' she answered coldly. 'I'm exactly like thousands of other women.'

They had drawn up in front of the house; he leant across her to open the door, but didn't open it. 'No, you're wrong; you're not like any other woman.' He opened the door at last, and said, 'By the way, isn't Bill Evans rather young for you?'

Sophy had been on the point of getting out, but she turned sharply in her seat, which was a mistake, for he was so near that her cheek brushed his. The touch made her catch her breath, but she managed to say in a tolerably calm voice, 'I've known Bill, for several months; I met you yesterday, Jonkheer van Oosterwelde. I can't think why it should be any business of yours nor why you should want to know anything about me… Goodnight.'

His voice came quietly through the gloom of the evening. 'Ah, yes, that is something else we must discuss, isn't it? Goodnight.'

She stood on the pavement, watching the big car disappear into the gathering twilight, her mouth slightly open. Presently she closed it with something of a snap, and went into the house. She had two days off; she was glad. It would be Saturday when she went back on duty, there were no lists on that day, only emergencies, and the RSO was on duty for the weekend. She wouldn't see the Dutchman until Monday.

Penny was waiting for her in the hall sitting on the stairs, school books scattered around her. She jumped up as Sophy shut the door.

'I heard a car—Sophy, did he bring you home? Was he waiting for you? How did he know where you were?' She paused for a much-needed breath, and sank back on to the bottom stair. 'Where does he come from?'

Sophy unbuttoned her jacket and sat down beside her sister, kicking off her shoes for greater comfort. She said in an unemotional voice. 'He's the surgeon who is relieving Uncle Giles while he goes on holiday.'

Penny leaned forward and hugged her sister. 'Sophy, how perfectly marvellous for you! Does he like you? Yes, of course he does—everyone likes you.' She interrupted herself. 'Uncle Giles on holiday again? But he's only just been a month or so ago. He and Aunt Vera came back in September, didn't they?'

Sophy chose to answer the second question first. 'Uncle Giles is ill—I expect we shall hear about it when we go there on Sunday. He and Aunt will be away for six weeks.'

Penny absorbed this information for a moment, then went doggedly back to her first question. 'You've not told me about the stranger—I still want to know. What's he like, and what is his name, and has he fallen for you?'

Sophy laughed. 'Oh, darling, no! He hardly spoke to me in theatre and he only brought me home because we happened to leave the hospital at the same time. He's a very good surgeon, I imagine, and his name is Professor Jonkheer Maximillan van Oosterwelde.' She laughed again at the expression on her sister's face.

'A professor,' said Penny, 'and with a name like that. He must be quite old; has he got grey hair?'

'Yes,' said Sophy. 'It's brushed very smoothly back without a parting and he's got a very high forehead, but his eyebrows are as black as thunder clouds. His eyes are pale blue...'

She stopped, aware of her sister's interested gaze, and got to her feet briskly. 'Bill's coming to supper on Saturday, so mind and have your homework done—you can't expect him to help you with your maths each time he comes, you know.'

Penny giggled. 'No, I know; but he's a dear, isn't he? He likes me too.' She stated the fact without conceit and added thoughtfully, 'I'm almost sixteen.'

Sophy said soberly, 'Yes, dear, and he's twenty-two and a very clever boy. In three years' time he'll know where he's going—and so will you.'

They smiled at each other, and Sophy thought, 'How strange, she's almost eleven years younger than I am and she knows who and what she wants already. I only hope Bill is sure enough to wait until she grows up.' She gave Penny a hug and said, 'Let's get supper. I'm off until Saturday; I think I shall go up to Harrods tomorrow and look around. You need a new coat for the winter—it's your turn, anyway. If I see anything you might like at our price, we'll go together next week and get it.'

They went off to the kitchen, happily engrossed in the rival merits of Irish tweed as opposed to a good hardwearing Harris.

Bill Evans arrived punctually for his supper, and was at once pounced upon and borne away to the shabby comfort of the small study at the end of the hall, where he good-naturedly corrected Penny's maths. They sat side by side at the desk, while he tried to make her understand the relations of the sides and angles of triangles. Sophy, coming to fetch them, thought how exactly right they were for each other; her pretty, sweet-natured young sister and this awkward, shy boy, who was yet man enough to hide his feelings behind a gentle teasing friendliness. It was strange, but he was never shy and awkward with Penny. Even Grandmother Greenslade, whose opinion of modern youth verged on the vituperative, approved of him; amending her opinion with the rider that Penny was still a schoolgirl and was to be treated as such.

Supper was a cheerful, rather noisy meal, with a great deal of talk. Even Sinclair, prowling in and out with second helpings, joined in from time to time, accompanied and hindered by the Blot and Titus, who liked to keep track of the food. The conversation was lively and varied, largely because the Greenslades had learned that without it life would be rather dull. There was no television in the house. Sophy had decided against it, and abetted by her grandmother, who disliked it very much, had managed to persuade the others that it was something they could do without, and an expense they couldn't afford to incur. There had been a little money when their parents died, but it was astonishing how fast it disappeared. Sophy had a fairly good salary and Grandmother Greenslade contributed her share; but only Sophy and perhaps Sinclair, who did most of the shopping, knew how carefully the money was budgeted.

They spent the evening playing Canasta and Sevens, and then Old Maid. Sophy hoped there was no significance in the fact that she was pronounced Old Maid time and time again.

She was on duty at eight o'clock on Sunday morning. There was no one about as she walked quickly to the hospital. It had been a quiet weekend in theatre so far. She hoped it would remain so, at least until she had had her free time that afternoon. She was off at one o'clock; she should be able to get to Uncle Giles by half past. She had two junior nurses on with her; they busied themselves turning out cupboards while she checked stock until they brought her coffee and went away to get their own. After they had gone the theatre was very quiet; Sophy pushed her books and forms and lists on one side, and sat rather despondently, doing nothing. Tom Carruthers, coming soft-footed into the little room, looked at her thoughtfully and said nothing. He accepted a mug of coffee and settled in the chair opposite hers. It was unlike Sophy to be down in the mouth, but he knew how fiercely independent she was, and he wasn't one to pry. Instead, he said, 'There's a nasty lot in Cas: femurs, tib and fib, fractured base—Orthopaedic will have their hands full. There's a nasty internal injuries too—not fit for anything yet, though. This evening at the earliest, I should think. You'll be on?'

Sophy nodded. 'Yes. I've a one to five—if I'm lucky. I'll be at Uncle Giles' as usual.'

'He's going on holiday; of course you know about it?' He raised an enquiring eyebrow. 'I must say it's a bit of luck getting that Dutch chap to do his work. Nice fellow too. Tall as Nelson's column and ten times as broad. Got a St Andrew's degree, too, as well as half a dozen Dutch ones. Met him yet?' He saw the pink stealing into Sophy's cheeks and looked out of the window.

'Yes, he's very good—he took the list on Wednesday.'

Tom passed his mug for more coffee. 'Quiet type, very amusing when he does talk, though—he's a baron or something of that sort.'

'A Jonkheer,' said Sophy before she could stop herself. She had been to the Reference Library on her day off and looked it up. 'It's an hereditary title.'

Tom gave her a sharp glance. 'Don't imagine he's the sort to broadcast it, though. Plenty of money, I hear. Drives a damn great Bentley too.'

Sophy looked suitably interested and was glad

when the telephone rang and a voice demanded Mr Carruthers. He listened to the urgent voice on the other end, and said,

'Oh, lord, Bill, just as I was going to dip into the Sunday papers. I'll be down.' He put down the receiver and turned to Sophy. 'A perf. Twenty minutes suit you? I'll go and check, but young Bill's pretty reliable.'

The morning's tempo changed. The smooth-running machinery of the theatre, never quite still, accelerated under Sophy's calm direction. The case came up, was dealt with, and was back in the ward by twelve-thirty.

It was almost an hour later when Sophy rang the door-bell of the nice old house where Mr Radcliffe had lived ever since she had known him. Matty, the elderly maid who opened the door, still wore the same kind of cap and apron she had worn when she had entered the surgeon's service almost three decades earlier. She looked prim, but smiled warmly at Sophy, and said, as she always said each Sunday,

'Just in time, Miss Sophy; Cook's dishing up.'

Sophy smiled too and enquired with interested sympathy about Matty's bad leg while she took off her coat and gave it into her keeping. Left alone, she went over to the old-fashioned mirror hanging on one wall and peered into it. She looked at her face with some dissatisfaction, anchored her hair more securely, and ran a licked finger over the smooth arches of her brows.

'Gilding the lily?' enquired a voice; the Dutchman's voice.

Sophy jumped, and at the same time was deeply

thankful that she was wearing a jersey shirtwaister that suited her admirably. She turned to face him as casually as she was able.

'You shouldn't take people by surprise like that,' she said severely. 'It's bad for their nerves.' Her voice was commendably steady, even though her pulse was not.

He made no effort to move, so that she was forced to remain where she was, looking up at him. He looked her over slowly and said, 'Very nice,' and then, 'Did you not expect me here?' His blue eyes searched hers. 'No, I see that you didn't. Your Uncle Giles is my Uncle Giles too, you know.'

Sophy tried to think of something to say; something clever or witty or charming; she was unable to think of anything at all, and, what was worse, she was only too aware that he knew it. She looked up to meet his quizzical gaze.

'Your aunt sent me to fetch you,' he said quietly. 'Are you ready?'

They crossed the hall in silence while Sophy turned over in her mind his remark about gilding the lily. He had been mocking her, of course; she had no illusions about her face.

As he opened the door he said on a laugh, just loud enough for her to hear, 'I do believe that no one has ever called you a lily before.'

He flung the door wide, and she went in to greet the politely impatient people waiting for their luncheon.

The table around which the company settled themselves was a large mahogany masterpiece, fashioned to accommodate a dozen persons at least. Sophy found herself beside Uncle Giles; Max van Ooster-welde was at the other end of the table next to Aunt Vera, with Penny on his other side. It was apparent that they were already the best of friends. She turned her head away and concentrated on her godfather, who was carving beef with a skill which was to have been expected of him.

Sophy passed the plates, and asked, soft-voiced in the general hum of conversation, where he and her aunt were going for their holiday.

'Dorset, my dear. Max has a nice little place tucked away down there—uses it when he comes to England. We've got the run of it for as long as we like. We shall leave here tomorrow. Later on, we hope to go over and stay with him in Holland, but that depends on how long I take to recoup and how long he can stay over here.'

He saw her anxious look and said quickly, 'Don't worry, my dear. It's nothing desperate—my heart's overdoing it a bit, that's all. Nothing a good rest won't cure.'

Sophy raised her eyes to his. 'Is that the truth, Uncle Giles, or are you busy pulling wool over my eyes?'

He laughed. 'The truth, girl. I've never lied to you, and don't intend to start now.' He finished his carving and sat down and helped himself to the dishes Matty was holding.

'Can I do anything to help you or Aunt Vera?'

He shook his head. 'No, my dear. At least, you might keep a motherly eye on Max.'

Sophy choked on a morsel of beef. 'A motherly eye on him?' she asked faintly.

'Yes. Though if you prefer it, I'll ask him to keep a fatherly eye on you.' He laughed so richly that everyone looked at him. He beamed at them all. 'Sophy and I are enjoying a joke together.' He winked broadly at her and turned to her grandmother, then left her to get on with her lunch.

After lunch Aunt Vera and Grandmother Greenslade wandered off to the drawing room, for what they called their weekly chat, and Uncle Giles bore Max van Oosterwelde away to his study, saying over his shoulder that there were plenty of apples for the picking at the end of the garden. Penny and Benjamin needed no second bidding, and tore away, followed more sedately but Sophy. Ten minutes later, however, sedateness forgotten, she was sitting astride a convenient fork in a tree, with a basket half filled on her arm, and a half eaten apple in her hand. It was pleasant there; the autumn sun still had warmth; the apples smelled good. She sighed, thinking how nice it would be to be free preferably driving about the country in a shining Bentley. It was only a small step from thinking of the Bentley to its owner; that was why his voice, coming from beneath her, sent the ready colour pouring over her face.

'Are these your shoes?' he asked.

Sophy curled her toes inside her stockings. 'Yes. I was afraid I'd spoil them.'

'Come down and put them on, and I'll get the rest of the apples for you, shall I?'

Penny and Benjamin had joined him, laden with their own spoils. She whisked down the old tree, in-

tent on getting to the ground unaided. She should
have known better. She was plucked from it while
she was still some feet from the ground, and set
lightly on her feet. Then he was gone, and a moment
later, she saw him balanced on a sturdy branch, reaching above his head and throwing the apples down to
them. He looked enormous, but somehow not in the
least out of place. The apples safely stowed, they went
back to the drawing room, where Uncle Giles had
switched on the television. He was following the incredible activities of a cowboy, apparently holding off
a mob of howling Indians single-handed. He took his
eyes from the screen long enough to recommend them
to sit down and watch too, and soon there was silence,
broken only by the sounds of celluloid battle. The
telephone brought a discordant note amongst the war
cries. Uncle Giles frowned, and turned the sound
down, and Sophy, who was nearest, picked up the
receiver. It was Staff Nurse.

'Sister, I thought you'd want to know that the internal injuries is coming up at five-thirty, but Cas rang
through to say they've got an abdominal that might
have to be done first. They've had a road accident in,
and Mr Carruthers is there now.'

Sophy looked at her watch; it was almost half past
four. 'Lay up for an abdominal, Cooper, and put in
the general set and all we need for nephrectomy and
splenectomy, and remember they'll probably want to
do an intravenous pyelogram.' She thought for a moment. 'And a few bladder tools, too. Have you got
Vincent there?'

Staff's voice came briskly back. 'Yes, Sister. She's
been to tea.'

'Good, tell her to get your tea now, before you dish up. I'll be with you very shortly. Goodbye.'

Before she could hang up, Pratt's voice cut in. 'Sister Greenslade, Mr Carruthers wants a word with you.'

Tom's quiet voice sounded urgent. 'Sophy, is Max van Oosterwelde there?'

She looked across the room; the big Dutchman was sprawled in a chair, watching her. She beckoned him, and said, 'Yes.' He took the telephone from her and she went to slip away, but he caught her by the hand.

'No, stay. It probably concerns you too.'

He listened quietly, and said at length, 'We'd better do her first. We'll be back in five minutes. No, not at all; I'm glad I can help. You've enough to get on with, I imagine.'

He was still holding her hand, she tried not to notice it while he talked. 'There's a girl in. Twelve years old—she's been stabbed. Carruthers says there are six entries in the abdomen for a start. He's got his hands full with the RTA. We'll do the girl first; she'll be a long job, I expect, but they can keep the other case going until we're ready.' He had been speaking quietly, so that only she could hear. Now he got up and went over to Mr Radcliffe. By the time Sophy had got her coat, he was saying goodbye in the unhurried manner of a man who had business to do, and knew how he was going to do it. As she made her own hurried goodbyes, she could hear him telling Penny and Ben that he would call for them on the following Wednesday. She longed to know more about it, but there was no time. They went round to the garage at the side of the house, and got into the Bentley and drove rapidly through the quiet streets. He left the car outside the hospital and they went in together, he to Cas, she to hurry upstairs to theatre. A few minutes later, capped and masked, she was scrubbing up while Cooper dished up the last of the instruments. They had five minutes. Vincent, the junior nurse, was nervous but willing; Staff, Sophy knew, would be a tower of strength; she always was. She went over to her trolleys and checked them carefully, and set about threading her needles and getting the blades on to their handles. It suddenly struck her that she didn't know who would be assisting. Carruthers was tied up in Cas.; the other two consultants had weekends; their houseman would probably be away too, leaving their patients to the care of whoever was on duty. The porters wheeled in the trolley, with Dr Walker, the senior anaesthetist, pushing the Boyles. He said 'Hullo, Sister' in a vague voice, and went back to his cylinders and tubes. She liked him very much; he was unflappable and very sure of himself.

The surgeons came in; the second one was Bill, looking excited and a little scared. She smiled at him behind her mask, and nothing of it showed except the little laughter lines round her beautiful eyes. He took the sponge holders she was holding out to him, and used them, and then waited while Max van Oosterwelde examined the small body between them. The wounds were hard to see, and for every one there would be two or three internally. When he'd finished he said,

'Have they got the fiend who did this?'

'Yes, sir. Her stepbrother. He says she had thrown

away his drugs and he was suffering from mental stress…'

The professor's eyes blazed and he said something in Dutch. Sophy thought it sounded like a good earthy Dutch oath—which it was. He put out a hand without looking at Sophy, and said, 'Ready, Sister.' She handed him the knife and he stood, relaxed, almost casual, with it in his hand.

'We'll do a lower right paramedian, shall we, and see how far we get?'

He was looking at Bill; accepting him as a partner. The boy looked back at him, flushing slightly. He'd been scared stiff until that moment; now, suddenly, he knew that he'd be all right.

It took two and a half hours; it wasn't a job to hurry over. Van Oosterwelde kept up a steady flow of quiet talk, and Sophy watched Bill relaxing under the older man's skilful guidance, until he was playing his full part.

They were checking swabs, and the two men stood quietly while Sophy counted and agreed the total with Nurse Vincent.

'How is your end, Walker?' asked van Ooster-welde; he was already busy with the mattress stitches.

'Very nice—she must be a tough little thing—she'll need some more blood, though. How much longer do you want?'

'Five minutes.' Bill cut the gut for him, and he threw the needle back on to Sophy's trolley. He caught her eye as he did so, and said, 'We didn't get our tea, did we?'

She handed him the Michel clip holder, but he waved it away towards Bill, and pulled off his gloves.

Sophy smiled behind her mask; he had been very kind to Bill. She called Vincent over and asked her to take a tray of tea to her office. Dr Walker and van Oosterwelde were standing together, looking down at the child's face.

'I'd like to wring that fellow's neck,' Dr Walker sounded vehement.

'I've got one of my own,' he added, 'so I feel strongly about it.'

The Dutchman said softly, 'I also would kill him, but,' he added, 'he will be sent to an institution for observation, and in five or ten years' time, he will do the same thing again.' He turned around, and cast a casual eye on Bill's work. 'Very nice,' he commented.

The second case took as long as the first, for it involved a splenectomy as well as a nephrectomy. Despite a hastily-snatched cup of tea, Sophy was tired. She had sent Vincent off duty, and Cooper was doing her own work and Vincent's too. The night staff were far too thinly stretched to borrow any of their number. The Orthopaedic theatre was still going, so was Cas. They would manage; they always did. It was close on eleven as the patient was wheeled back to Intensive Care. The men followed him down; they wanted to look at the girl as well. Sophy and Cooper plunged into the chaos of used instruments and needles and knives, while a night porter swabbed up. It was almost an hour later when the two girls parted company at the end of the theatre corridor. Sophy slipped quiet as a mouse through the dim corridors, and down the stairs, calling a soft goodnight to the porter as she passed his box, and so through the big

swing doors. Jonkheer van Oosterwelde was on the
top step, leaning against its iron balustrade. He took
her arm lightly above her elbow, and they went down
the steps together and into the big car. She sat back
against its leathered comfort and let out a tired breath.

'Are they all right?' she asked, as he moved away
from the kerb. 'Have you been there all this time?'
And blushed at her question.

'I'm not sure about the girl—the man's all right for
the moment. Do you always have to clear up after a
case at night? Don't the night staff help?'

She explained about the nurses having more than
enough to do and added, 'You weren't—that is, you
didn't wait for me, did you?'

He turned his head and looked at her. 'Yes.'

She waited for him to say something else, but he
remained silent, as he brought the car to a quiet halt
outside her home.

'Thank you very much, sir. It was very kind of
you.' Honestly compelled her to add, 'But I always
walk home by myself after a late case. I'm not lonely
or nervous.'

She put a hand on the door, but his came down to
hold it and prevent her.

'Is there someone at home to give you a hot drink?'

She gave a gurgle of tired laughter; saw his raised
eyebrow and said, 'I'm sorry; I wasn't being rude—
it's just that I've never met a senior consultant surgeon who bothered with things like hot drinks for
nurses. Everyone will be in bed, but Sinclair will have
left a thermos of cocoa for me...'

'Sinclair?'

She was really very tired, but she thought she had

better answer his question; he was the sort of man, she thought sleepily, who expected to be answered. 'He was my father's batman during the war. He came back with him afterwards and has been with us ever since. I've known him nearly all my life; he's a tower of strength and a friend and he's marvellous at housework too. He gave us the Blot, and he found Titus in a gutter; when my parents died, he made us keep on— it was a bit…difficult at first.'

He got out and came round and opened the door and walked up the little path with her, and took the door key from her hand and opened the door. There was a light in the hall. She went past him, and then turned on the step to look at him.

'Goodnight, sir.'

'Goodnight, Miss Greenslade. I made a mistake today. You do not need any gilding.'

She awoke early, after a short night of heavy sleep and ridiculous dreams about lilies. She went on duty determined to be sensible. She wasn't a silly young girl; she was a woman with responsibilities and not much time for romantic ideas. She was breathtakingly efficient in theatre during the morning, and at coffee time went on a mythical errand which lasted until it was time to scrub again. It was really quite easy to avoid being alone with him. She went to her dinner late, and went straight back to work. The list was an uncomplicated one that afternoon; they could be done by five, if they didn't stop for tea. There was one case left, when Jonkheer van Oosterwelde called a halt. Even then, she sent the nurse in with the tea tray, and elected to stay in theatre, although there was really nothing for her to do there. He appeared in the doorway five minutes later, smiled charmingly at the nurses and said in a silky voice it would have been hard to disobey:

'Your tea is getting cold, Sister.'

She had opened her mouth to tell him that she didn't want any tea, but the three nurses had all paused in their work and were watching with a lively interest that needed quelling. As she went ahead of him down the corridor she thought bitterly, that he was the pin-up boy for practically the whole staff already, then hated herself for the thought. He had, after all, been very kind to her, and he had treated Bill decently. All the same, he was too sure of himself, too certain of getting his own way.

She went into the little office, and Dr Walker and Bill got up while she squeezed past them to sit in her chair. She was drawn at once into their conversation and was surprised to find how much she was enjoying it. Perhaps, after all, she need not avoid him—not when there were other people around. She became aware that Bill was speaking to her, and said,

'I'm sorry, Bill—I didn't hear you.'

He flushed faintly. 'I only wondered if you would mind if I took Penny to Hampton Court on Saturday afternoon.' His flush deepened; the other two men had stopped talking and were listening. 'I'll bring her back after tea,' he finished doggedly.

Sophy gave him a gentle smile. 'Of course you can, Bill. Stay to supper if you're off duty; you're the only one who can do her trig homework, anyway.'

He gave her a grateful look, and got up to take the tea tray back.

Sophy, aware that Jonkheer van Oosterwelde was looking at her intently, studied the off-duty chart on her desk, until she felt compelled to meet his gaze. Something in his expression made her lift her chin, and he chuckled. Kindly Providence, in the shape of Dr Walker, intervened.

'That boy'll make Penny a good husband one of these days,' he said comfortably. 'Not the sort to change his mind, either.' He looked at Sophy. 'About time you got settled, isn't it, Sophy? How old are you?' She didn't resent his questions; she had known him for years; he had always been outspoken. She answered without rancour.

'I've not found anyone who wants to settle with me, Dr Walker, and I'm twenty-six next birthday.'

'God bless my soul, you don't look it, Sophy. Luke will be finished in a couple of years, won't he? He should try for an appointment here and keep an eye on the others while you go off for a cruise...'

'A cruise, Dr Walker?' She burst out laughing. 'Oh, to find a husband. I'll think about it.' She got up. 'In the meantime, I'll get scrubbed.' She skipped through the door, avoiding van Oosterwelde's eye.

The list was finished for the day, and Sophy was sitting in her office, neat and fresh in her dark blue and white uniform, writing up the theatre book. The men had gone some time ago. The theatre was ready again for any emergency; Staff was in charge; she herself was going home as soon as she could get her books done. She heard the steps in the corridor, and when they stopped outside the door, she called, 'Come in,' and as the door opened said, 'Now don't tell me, there's an appendix in and you'd like to...'

She looked up. The professor was leaning in the doorway, his head carefully bent to avoid the door frame; the very epitome of a well-dressed gentleman of leisure.

He stayed where he was and said, 'Are you not off duty, Sister?'

Sophy frowned. 'Yes,' she said shortly, 'I am, but I have books and things to fill in. I can't do them in the theatre,' she said with heavy sarcasm.

He looked indifferent. She shot a cross look at him, thinking that probably he thought she was inefficient.

'I'll not take up your time then. I wished merely to say that I have asked Penny and Benjamin to come out with me on Wednesday afternoon. It wasn't until I heard young Evans asking your permission to take Penny out that I realised that I should do the same.'

Sophy, listening to his cool voice, thought that he made her sound like a fussy aunt. It was her day off on Wednesday, too; she determined then and there to go away for the day—for the whole day, until quite late, so that there was no chance of meeting him. She raised a cheerfully polite face to his.

'How kind of you,' she said warmly. 'They'll love it.' She allowed her hand to hover over the telephone, and he saw the gesture as he was meant to, and wished her a rather curt goodnight. She listened to his steps receding, and then got up slowly, said goodnight to Staff, and walked in her turn down the corridor to change, and go home.

CHAPTER THREE

IT WAS striking ten as Sophy let herself into the house on Wednesday evening. True to the promise she had made herself, she had gone out just before lunch; spent the afternoon with Tom Carruthers' wife, stretching her visit for as long as good manners allowed, and then walked most of the way home. Even then it had been far too early, and she had been forced to spend a long hour drinking cups of coffee she didn't want, while she reflected on the waste of a precious day off.

The hall was dim and quiet. It smelled of polish and the tantalising post-prandial aroma of toasted cheese. She felt her appetite sharpen, and went straight to the kitchen. Sinclair always made tea for himself before bedtime; she would have one with him and enquire about the cheese; there might be some left. Sinclair looked up as she went into the cosy, old-fashioned room and jumped to his feet.

'Thought you might be in, Miss Sophy,' he said. 'How about a nice cuppa, and there's a slice of Quiche Lorraine I've kept warm.' He pushed the elderly arm chair by the Aga invitingly in her direction. 'Sit down.'

Sophy did as she was bid, tossing her hat and gloves on to the table.

'You're tired, Miss Sophy.' He handed her a plate,

and she picked up a fork and started to eat with a
healthy appetite.

'Yes, Sinclair.' She took a satisfying draught of the
black, syrupy tea Sinclair preferred. 'I wish I wasn't
plain,' she said, apropos of nothing at all. Sinclair
seemed to understand.

'You're not plain, Miss Sophy; you only think you
are, especially when you're tired or upset or down in
the dumps.'

She smiled at him. 'You are a dear, Sinclair. Did
the children have a nice trip?' she asked in a carefully
casual voice.

He nodded. 'They went to Canterbury.'

'Canterbury? But that's miles away.'

'Yes, miss, but not in a Bentley, it isn't. They went
all round the Cathedral and had a bang-up tea. They
were back by half-past six. This doctor, he stayed to
supper; very merry they were too. Helped Master Ben
with his Latin too.' He got up and put the cups in the
sink. 'They went to bed punctual, miss.'

Sophy got up and went slowly to the door. 'I'm
glad they enjoyed themselves,' she said tonelessly.
'Goodnight, Sinclair.'

Her grandmother was in the sitting room as she
went in. She looked up, pencil poised. 'Hullo, darling.
What's a fanatical artist making a bid?'

Sophy went and sat near the fire on a little velvet-
covered stool and held her nicely-kept hands out to
its warmth. 'Rabid,' she said. 'How are you, Granny?'

Her grandmother wrote rapidly. 'You're right, darling. How clever of you. Did you have a nice day?'
She didn't wait for an answer, but went on, 'The children had a lovely afternoon with Max...'

Sophy stirred. 'Max already,' she thought, and said out loud, 'How nice for them. They were back before supper, so Sinclair tells me.'

'Yes, dear. Max stayed; he looked lonely. We had Quiche Lorraine, and Sinclair made a lovely treacle tart—we saved some for you. Where was I? Oh, yes. Max ate a good supper, but he's a big man, isn't he? He helped Ben with his Latin...'

'It's like listening to a gramophone record,' thought Sophy, and at the same time waited eagerly for anything else her grandmother had to say. She wondered what it was about this man that could make Sinclair and her grandmother so interested in him—and me too, she added honestly. 'I've thought about him ever since I first saw him.'

'I wonder how old he is?' she mused.

'Thirty-nine, and not married. He lives close to a small river in Holland—it's pretty there, he said, and near Utrecht. He's a Senior Consulting Surgeon at a hospital there, and teaches the students, too. He's got a spaniel called Meg, and a bulldog called Jack.'

Mrs Greenslade paused to draw a much-needed breath, and Sophy said, 'Granny, what a lot you know about him.'

Her grandmother looked at her shrewdly. 'Nothing that he wouldn't have told you, if you'd asked him, my dear Sophy. I thought it would be nice if he lunched here on Sunday—it's your day off, isn't it?— I know you see him most days, but I don't suppose you get to know much about the people you work with in that theatre—why, I don't suppose you see the patients as people; just—something, under a lot of sterile sheets. And as for working there, how can you possibly get to know anybody when all you can see of them is their eyes?' She sounded indignant.

Sophy twisted round on her stool. 'It's not like that at all, Grandmother,' she cried. She was remembering the Dutch surgeon's face when he had bent over the little girl the previous Sunday. 'He...we all mind about the patients, and when we're working it's like a team.'

Her grandmother looked across at her. 'I'm glad to hear it, Sophy. I was beginning to think you didn't like Max.' She took no notice of her granddaughter's gasp. 'We'll have roast pork, I think, and follow it with a mince tart and cream, and Sinclair shall go to that funny little grocer's shop where there are all those cheeses. Men always like cheese,' she added. She took off her glasses, and looked ten years younger. 'I think I'll go to bed, I'm quite tired.' She didn't look in the least tired. She folded the newspaper carefully, so that the crossword was on top, ready for the morning, and got up. Sophy got up too, unwilling to be left alone with her thoughts. She wished Grandmother Greenslade a good night, and went upstairs to her room. Once there, she didn't undress but stood in front of the big, old-fashioned mirror, gazing intently at her face. It seemed to her that however she looked at it, it was still a plain one.

The next morning, she offered a surprised and delighted Cooper Sunday off in her place—Staff was so wrapped in her good luck that she lent only half an ear to Sophy's singularly thin reasons for wishing to make the change; which, thought Sophy, was just as well. Sophy said nothing at home until Saturday evening, and received the sympathetic remarks of her family with a quietness which they put down to her disappointment at missing Sunday luncheon. She was feeling horribly guilty, especially as Jonkheer van Oosterwelde had been so pleasant in theatre.

It was a fine morning as she walked to the hospital on Sunday. There was a blue sky and the sun shone, although there was no warmth in its rays, but Sophy's spirits did not match the morning; for all she cared, it could have been blowing a force nine gale, with rain to match.

She spent the first part of the morning in theatre, teaching the two junior nurses who were on duty with her. The place was in a state of readiness and uncannily quiet—their voices sounded strange against the emptiness of the big tiled room. After a time, she set the girls to cleaning instruments and went off to Orthopaedic theatre to have coffee with Sister Skinner; a lovely blonde who looked like a film star and fell in and out of love so frequently that Sophy had long ago given up trying to remember who the men were; but she was always prepared to lend a sympathetic ear while Skinner discussed her latest conquest. Inevitably, she wanted to know about the new surgeon.

'I must meet him,' she exclaimed. 'I saw him leaving the other day; he didn't see me,' she added, 'or he might have stopped.'

Sophy chuckled. 'Of course he'd have stopped...'

Skinner put down her coffee. 'Sophy, ring me when you have a coffee break on Monday—you've got a list, haven't you? We haven't. I'll pop over and borrow something, then you can introduce me.' She looked at Sophy with a puzzled frown. 'Is he as nice as he looks?'

Sophy nodded. 'Oh, yes. He's very good at his job, and he never loses his needle or throws swabs on the floor...'

'Silly, I didn't mean his work. Look, Sophy, he's good-looking and distinguished and a marvellous surgeon—if I'd been in your shoes I'd have been out to dinner with him by now.'

Sophy laughed. 'I know you would; but I'm not you, my dear. You're so pretty men look at you and want to take you out—but if you were a man, would you look twice at me?' She spoke without rancour as she got up to go. 'I'll ring you about eleven on Monday. Tom Carruthers will be assisting; I'll get him out of the way, and leave you alone to exercise your charms.'

She called in on Casualty on her way back, but although it was full, there was nothing for the theatre. She sent the nurses to their dinner, and went into her office and started on her books, but after a few minutes she got up again, and stood by the window, watching the coming and going in the inner courtyard below. She was just turning away, when she caught sight of Bill Evans and Max van Oosterwelde strolling through the archway from X-Ray. They were deep in discussion, although Bill seemed to be doing most of the talking; he was a tall young man, but the Dutchman dwarfed him. Half way across the yard, they met Tom Carruthers, and stopped. She wondered what they could be talking about; nothing serious, for there was a good deal of laughter. Anyway, Jonkheer van Oosterwelde wasn't on call; she supposed he'd come in to see someone. He looked up suddenly, and although he was too far away for her to be sure of his expression, she was sure that he frowned when he saw her. She backed away from the window—how awful to be caught peeping. She went into the theatre, and prowled around moving things that didn't need moving, and after a few minutes went back to her office again, and peeped cautiously from the window. He had gone. She got out the instrument catalogue and started to make a list of replacements, but her heart wasn't in it. She was contemplating an excellent illustration of Syme's aneurism needle with little more than tepid interest, when she heard the faint squeak of the swing doors at the end of the corridor. It wouldn't be the nurses; they had only been gone ten minutes or so; and the third year nurse wasn't due on until one o'clock. She sat up straight—it was a man's tread, and she knew whose tread it was. She quelled a strong urge to rearrange her cap and do something to her face, and waited, hands in lap, with her eyes to the door.

He came in without knocking, closed the door behind him, stood with his back to it, and said without preamble, 'What have I done?'

Sophy's lovely eyes opened wide, framed by the curling sweep of black lashes; her mouth was open too; she closed it with something of a snap, and blinked. 'I don't think I quite understand,' she faltered.

Max van Oosterwelde left the door and settled himself in the chair opposite hers. He was wearing tweeds—unobtrusive, superbly cut, and she thought, wildly expensive. He stretched out a long arm and took the off-duty rota from the desk.

'You had a day off today; you changed it, and don't

give me any nonsense about Staff Nurse wanting it—she told me about it on Friday.'

He grinned wickedly, and Sophy, choking on rage, didn't mince her words.

'You have no right to…to…' She caught his eye.

'To what?' he enquired silkily.

'The nurses' off-duty is no concern of yours.' She remembered who he was, and added, 'Sir.'

'No, it's not, but we stray from the point, do we not? You took care to be away from home last Wednesday. I had dinner with the Carruthers, you know; you left there soon after five; you weren't home when I left at nine. I thought maybe you were out with a boyfriend; and then I heard that you had changed your duty today, and it seemed more than coincidence and that you had done it deliberately. Do you dislike me so much, Sophy?'

Sophy dragged her gaze away from the waste paper basket, and gave him a level look. 'I don't dislike you.' Her voice was quiet and faintly surprised.

'Then I suggest you drop your guard, my girl. I've no intention of laying violent hands on you, nor,' he went on deliberately, 'am I interested in flirting with you.' He watched her face flame with a detached air. 'I see no reason why we shouldn't be friends, do you? After all, we share a godfather—that is surely a sound enough motive for friendship?'

She met his eyes and saw that he was smiling. She ignored her heart bouncing against her ribs, and said in an even little voice, 'I'm afraid I've become a real old maid in the last few years.' She managed a very credible smile, and put a hand in the one he was holding out. His clasp was firm and comforting. She needed comfort, but he wouldn't know that, of course.

'No, never that—old maids don't climb trees.'

He relinquished her hand, and picked up the telephone and asked for Matron.

Sophy listened to the conversation, and it was at once apparent to her that he was going to get his own way, although she doubted if Matron would realise it. He put down the receiver and got up.

'Ten past one at the front door? You'll have to keep your uniform on, I'm afraid, just in case they need you in a great hurry. Don't be late—I promised Mrs Greenslade we would be there by a quarter past one.'

Sophy looked at him with raised eyebrows. 'You promised Granny...' her eyes searched his face. 'But they're not expecting me.'

He was halfway through the door. 'Yes, they are. I forgot to mention that I telephoned your grandmother and told her that you would be home for luncheon.'

She frowned. 'Well, really!' she exploded. She stopped; he had already gone.

He sat next to Mrs Greenslade at luncheon, and carved the joint as well if not better than Uncle Giles would have done. Sophy saw that he was on the friendliest terms with Penny and Benjamin, and it was obvious that her grandmother had been completely won over. Even Sinclair, who took his dislikes and likes seriously, approved of him. They had their coffee around the sitting room's bright fire, surrounded by the Sunday papers and Penny's discarded knitting and a half-finished jig-saw puzzle Ben had tired of. Mrs Greenslade sat on one side of the fire, her current crossword on her lap, and the enormous dictionary she was never without serving its dual purpose as a foot-stool. Jonkheer van Oosterwelde occupied the chair opposite her, with the Blot pressed hard against one knee, half-shut eyes expressing the bliss of having his ears rubbed. Titus had spread himself across the Dutchman's well polished shoes, ignoring the offers of a lap from the other occupants of the room.

Sophy, curled up in a corner of the couch said, 'Isn't it extraordinary, how they like you? They're usually so fussy.'

She saw his lips twitch and his dark brows lift, and blushed and said hastily, 'Oh, I didn't mean to be rude, I'm sorry, but you must know what I mean. Perhaps it's because they sense you've got dogs of your own.'

'Very probably,' he replied, 'though I would prefer to think that it was good taste on their part.'

Amid the general laughter, Penny asked, 'Don't they miss you while you're away; your animals, I mean?'

'Yes, very much, I believe, but they have plenty of friends, and I think that the welcome I receive is largely an act.'

Sophy glanced at her watch, and got up reluctantly. Her grandmother gave her a smooth cheek to kiss and said,

'Must you go, darling?—such a shame when we're all so cosy. Anyway, I hope you have a nice afternoon,' she added vaguely. Max had risen too, and was already at the door. 'Don't be long, Max,' she called as they went out.

They didn't talk on the short trip to the hospital;

there wasn't time anyway. Sophy thanked him briefly
as she got out, and ran up the hospital steps without
looking back. Half an hour later, she was scrubbing
up beside Tom Carruthers; there was a nasty face injuries in—too serious for Cas to deal with. It was no
sooner on the table than the telephone rang; there was
an acute obstruction just in and perhaps Mr Carruthers
would go and see him as soon as he could. Tom Carruthers growled something under his breath, and Sophy sent the nurse back with a polite message to say
that he would be down as soon as he could manage
it. It turned out to be one of those afternoons when
there could be no pause for tea; the obstruction took
a long time, and it was almost six o'clock by the time
they had finished and Tom and Dr Walker had followed the porters out of the theatre. Sophy and the
two nurses on duty cleared up with the speed of long
use, and she sent them to supper while she sat in the
quiet theatre, doing the needles, her mind full of the
little girl Max van Oosterwelde had operated upon the
week before. Tom had told her quietly, as he left the
theatre, that the child had died. 'Van Oosterwelde saw
her this morning,' he had said, 'but there was nothing
he could do. Decent of him to come in, though. After
all, it was his day off, and he didn't get to bed until
four am—been out on the town.' Sophy sorted the
last of the needles, and tried not to remember that
remark. It could mean so many things. She shook her
neat head as though to shake the thought away. It was
none of her business, anyway, but she couldn't stop
herself reflecting on the number of very pretty girls
on the nursing staff who would doubtless make ex-

cellent companions for a man who wished to go out on the town.

She got up and tidied away the bits and pieces, and when the nurses came back from supper, sent them off duty. She would be going home herself very soon. In a little while, she switched off the lights and went along to change.

The Bentley slid to the kerb as she reached the pavement. The door opened, and Max's voice said quietly, 'Get in.'

She hadn't expected it. She managed a rather breathless Hallo and sat wordlessly beside him. The street door was open as they reached the house, and he got out too, and followed her up the little path. Penny came out of the kitchen as they went in.

'There you are,' she cried. 'I've cooked the most delicious supper, and Max has brought a bottle of wine.'

He shut the door behind them and said, with a chuckle, 'I'm by way of being a lodger today. I hope you don't mind?'

Sophy smiled. 'No, of course I don't.'

His eyes searched her face. 'You're tired—were you busy?'

She told him, and he said slowly, 'You're not tired—you're upset or sad, aren't you?'

Sophy turned to go into the sitting room. 'Yes, a little, but don't let's talk about it...'

'We'll talk about it now,' he said quietly. He had put a detaining hand on her shoulder, and left it there. 'You heard about our little patient.'

'Tom Carruthers told me this evening. I...' she

drew a deep breath. 'It's so unfair; she was only a child.'

He laid a gentle hand on her other shoulder, and turned her round to face him. 'But sickness and accidents and death are all unfair, aren't they?' he asked. 'Isn't that why we ply our particular trades?' he ran a finger up her cheek; his touch was very comforting to her. 'Surely our calm, unruffled Miss Greenslade isn't beaten? Each time this happens, it's a challenge.'

Sophy stood still, feeling the pressure of his hands on her shoulders, stiffling a mad longing to cast herself on to his broad chest and howl her eyes out. She dismissed this absurd notion, and said steadily, 'You're quite right; you mostly are, I think. Thank you for understanding.'

He smiled slowly. 'That's better.'

He took his hands away, and caught her by the elbow and steered her towards the sitting room. 'A glass of sherry, I think, before we face whatever Penny has in store for us.'

Penny had surpassed herself with a mushroom omelette, chips and Daisy chicory. Max van Oosterwelde speared the last piece of mushroom, and said, 'That was—er—super, Penny. One day, you will make an excellent wife.'

Penny glowed. 'Yes, I think I shall,' she said seriously. 'Have you a wife, Max?'

He didn't answer at once; there was time for Sophy's sharp 'Penny!' before he said quietly, 'No, not yet.'

Penny ignored her sister's frown, and persisted, 'Well, you'd better hurry up and get married, hadn't

you, or you won't have time to enjoy your children—
No, Sophy, I won't be quiet; Max is our friend, and
I want him to be happy,' She turned her attention to
him once more. 'You'll want a son to take over your
practice when you retire, you know. That's what
Daddy was going to do with Luke...' There was a
little pause; even after four years, they weren't quite
used to being orphans.

Max said quickly, bridging the awkward moment,
'That's a great deal of good advice, Penny. I think I
must take it.'

'Are you engaged?' began Benjamin, but Sophy
had had enough.

'Ben, even the closest friends don't ask questions
of each other they might not wish to answer.'

Ben smiled disarmingly. 'Sorry. But is it all right
if I ask you why you don't call Max by his name?
He said we could days ago, and he calls you Sophy,
don't you, Max? I've heard you.'

The Dutchman had been sitting back in his chair,
watching the boy with a half-smile on his face. Now
he stirred and said, 'Er—yes, I do, Benjamin, but in
hospital I have to remember to say Sister.'

'Well, yes, I can understand that—what does Sophy call you there?'

Max laughed. 'Sir, and when I'm being particularly
trying—asking for tea at the wrong time, or forgetting
to give her instruments that I've finished with, and
things of that sort, she calls me Jonkheer van Oosterwelde in a stern voice which brings me to heel very
quickly indeed.'

Everyone laughed at the very idea of Sophy being
stern, and Ben quite forgot to get an answer to his

question, and a moment later Max got up to go, and said his thanks and goodbyes amid a burst of cheerful talk. He went first to Mrs Greenslade and kissed her hand, which action, done with obvious sincerity, caused her to turn pink and bridle. He said quietly, for her ears only, 'I'm free on Tuesday: will you give me the pleasure of taking you out to lunch?'

Grandmother opened her still beautiful eyes wide and looked startled. 'Me?' she said. 'Do you mean me?'

He lifted black brows in faint puzzlement. 'Who else should I ask? Would Wiltons suit you, do you think?'

She was looking at him steadily, and appeared to like what she saw. 'That will be delightful. Thank you, Max.'

'Good, I'll call for you about twelve-thirty.'

He turned to leave, fending off the Blot and Titus, who showed a desire to accompany him. Sophy had somehow drifted to the other end of the room. She responded cheerfully to his goodnight, and set about clearing away the supper things. Penny and Benjamin washed up, for Sinclair wouldn't be in until late, while she and her grandmother debated the important question of clothes suitable for a luncheon date. It was only after she had got ready for bed and turned out the light that she allowed her own private thoughts to take over. She went carefully over the day. Max had asked for her friendship, but that was all. Going over the conversations they had had, she could not find a single word that would allow her to hope otherwise.

CHAPTER FOUR

MONDAY WAS COLD and wet. Sophy, who had laddered a stocking and burnt the porridge was not her usual sweet-tempered self. There was a new nurse on duty in theatre for the first time too; a slim, graceful creature, who was quite obviously shrinking from work she didn't fancy. Sophy, shrouding her cross little face in her theatre cap and mask, thought darkly that the girl would need bolstering up and calming down, and careful handling. She would probably faint and collapse on to a sterile trolley.

There was no one scrubbing yet. Sophy started on the careful, rather tedious task soberly, going carefully over the theatre list as she did so. She must remember to arrange coffee as near eleven as possible because of Mary Skinner, and she must let Staff know, so that she could ring her up and give her time to get over. The first two cases would be fairly long ones; they could probably get a break after the second one. Her thoughts were interrupted by a resounding crash from the theatre. She sighed, put down the brush, and popped her head round the door. Robins, the new girl, had knocked over a sterile bowl stand. Sophy eyed the trembling creature, paddling about on a floor glistening wetly with its unexpected douching, and said in a quiet, kind voice with just the right amount of briskness in it,

'All right, Nurse, it's not as bad as it looks.' She

transferred her calm gaze to the other junior nurse. 'Nurse Winters, show Nurse where we keep the mop and bucket, and mop up between you, and be quick about it.'

She heard Staff's familiar tread behind her, and said thankfully, 'Ah, Staff Nurse. See that they clear up that mess, will you, and dish a couple more bowls.' She added, 'Thank heaven she did it now, and not half an hour later.' With which muddled remark, Staff readily agreed.

Back in the scrub room, she turned on the taps once more. For the first time in years, she felt a lack of enthusiasm for her work. Perhaps she was getting stale, or tired—a useless supposition when she still had another thirty years to go. She contemplated a seemingly endless vista of theatre cases, scrubbing up and training nurses, getting, she assumed, crabbier each year. She stood, brush poised, appalled. The door swung open, and Max van Oosterwelde walked in. He wished her a correct good morning in a cool voice and went over to the sink furthest from her, where he started to scrub, taking no notice of her. He was capped and masked and trousered in the usual white drill reach-me-down trousers. He hitched up his rubber apron before he began, and Sophy, watching him warily sideways, thought that he looked exactly what he was; a member of that out-of-date community—the ruling class. Perhaps they still had such a thing in Holland; she didn't know. He turned his head and caught her gaze before she could look away. It was a haughty enquiring look; it made her feel as though she had been reading his letters, or listening at a keyhole. She went scarlet behind her mask, and attacked her already well scrubbed hands with a quite unnecessary vigour, while her heart thumped and her breath fluttered out of control. Only when she had both these under command did she allow herself to face up to the discovery she had just made. She was, heaven help her, head over heels in love with Professor Jonkheer van Oosterwelde. She said out loud, 'Oh, dear. What now?'

She took her gown from her marked drum, and stood obediently while the nurses tied her tapes. It was while she was putting on her gloves that he said casually over one shoulder,

'When we have the leisure, you shall explain that remark to me.'

Sophy adjusted a rubber cuff with a faintly shaking hand. 'Indeed I will not, sir,' she said in a level little voice. She turned away, wished Tom and Bill a cheerful good morning as they came in to scrub, and went her way into theatre.

Sophy had judged her times very well; it was just eleven o'clock when the second case left the theatre. She nodded to Nurse Winters to fetch the coffee tray, and went down the corridor to her office, the three men close behind. Mary was already there, sitting on the edge of the desk, swinging a nicely turned leg. She stayed there just long enough for the Dutchman to appreciate this fact, then jumped down, settling the belt round her shapely waist, and smiling charmingly at him across the little room.

She said, without taking her beautiful blue eyes from his, 'Sophy, I'm right out of Oxycel. Could you possibly let me have some, just in case something turns up before I can get any?'

Sophy stood by the door, admiring her friend's technique. She couldn't see Max, he was just behind her, but surely Mary would have a conquest—she always did. She went a little further into the room, and said, 'Of course, Mary—I'll fetch it in a minute; but have coffee with us first. I don't think you have met Professor van Oosterwelde yet, have you?'

She half turned, and caught his eye. He was smiling charmingly at Sister Skinner, but she was surprised to see his eyes alight with amusement. 'This is Sister Mary Skinner, Orthopaedic Theatre Sister, sir.'

She watched them shake hands and admitted to herself that they made a striking pair, who became at once immersed in the sort of witty, frothy conversation which she could never quite manage. She sat down and poured the coffee; it was nice that Tom and Bill were there. She drank her coffee quickly and to Bill's astonishment, asked him to go to the cubbyhole for more hot milk. She thrust a nearly full jug into his hands, with such a fierce frown that he put his own half-drunk coffee down, and went away protesting. She gave him half a minute, then got up herself. At the door, she said, 'Oh, Mr Carruthers, I want your advice about something; I've got the catalogue out here, would you come and have a look?'

She gave him a speaking glance from her lovely eyes, and hiding a smile, he got up too. 'I'll come now,' he said easily. And when they were outside in the corridor, 'What are you up to, Sophy.'

'Skinner wants a date,' said Sophy in a conspirator's whisper.

Tom Carruthers stifled a laugh. 'Good lord, you women! None of us is safe.'

'Don't be silly,' Sophy replied. 'Mary's pretty, and great fun. They'll have a lovely time together.' It was like twisting a knife in a wound.

Tom shook his head. 'She's not his type,' he said. Sophy pounced. 'What's his type?' she asked. She wasn't looking at Tom as she spoke, and he didn't answer her question anyway. Instead, he asked, 'Where's this mythical catalogue?'

She produced it from a windowsill where she had had the forethought to put it, and went off to get the Oxycel. On her way back, she looked in the anaesthetic room. The next patient was already there; Dr Walters, who hadn't wanted any coffee, was drawing up Pentothal. He smiled at her, and said, 'Ten minutes, Sophy?'

She nodded, said, 'Yes; of course, Dr Walters,' and sped away. Mary had had ten minutes, ample time to get her date, judging by what she had seen of her methods. She went back to the office, thinking how strange it was that she could think about Mary spending an evening with Max, and not mind about it. She felt curiously numb; she wondered how she would feel later on, when she had time to sit down and think. They turned to look at her as she went in: Mary with an expression akin to relief, Max blankly from ice blue eyes. Sophy handed over the Oxycel, which Mary took with feverish thanks. The two girls went out of the room together, and the door was barely shut behind them before Mary burst out.

'Do you know what we talked about?' She turned a bewildered face to Sophy. 'Delayed primary suturing. He…he held forth. I didn't have a chance to say a word, and he didn't even look at me; just a cold glance once in a while to make sure I was listening. He'd be a wasted evening,' she finished, rather pettishly.

Sophy expressed sympathy, for she had the sort of nature that was incapable of doing otherwise, and walked back towards the scrubbing room. At her office door, she paused, then opened it. Van Oosterwelde had his back to her. He didn't turn round, but said quietly, 'Come in and shut the door.'

Sophy did as she was bid, looking lovingly at his broad back; it looked somehow annoyed. She glanced at the clock—probably he was going to tick her off for lingering over coffee break.

He turned round suddenly, and she altered her expression, so that she presented her usual calm appearance. He gave her a hard stare. 'Your friend is a very pretty young woman,' he said.

Sophy nodded brightly. 'Yes, isn't she? She's the prettiest girl in the hospital. We're good friends,' she added, just in case he was unaware of the fact.

'I lectured her about primary sutures.'

Sophy lifted puzzled eyes to his. 'Yes, she told me.' She paused. 'Didn't you like her?'

His eyes glinted—was it rage or laugher? It was impossible to tell.

'My dear girl, I had no idea that you would take Penny's advice to me so much to heart—I'm deeply touched; but you see I'm not—er—available. Is that the right word?'

Sophy felt her heart twist and then plummet down to her feet. Her common sense told her that such a thing was not possible; nevertheless, the sensation was a very unpleasant one. She drew a long slow breath, and answered steadily, 'Available isn't quite the right word, but I understand perfectly what you mean.'

He looked suddenly quite cheerful, and said, 'I wonder if you do...' He broke off as Tom put his head round the door. 'Ready when you are, sir,' he said crisply.

Sophy whisked past him and into the scrubbing room. What had Max been going to say? She thought about it for perhaps twenty seconds, and then, like the good nurse she was, deliberately shut her mind to everything but her work.

She was glad that they were so busy for the rest of the day that there was no time for anything but necessary talk. Soon after five, the four men went away together, calling casual goodnights as they went. Sophy went home too, nearly an hour later, and this time there was no one on the top step waiting for her.

The following day was busy too; and it seemed the more so to her after an almost sleepless night—she might just as well have slept soundly for all the help it had been to the muddled thoughts milling around inside her usually sensible little head. The day seemed endless, and very dull without Max in the theatre, and when she eventually got home it was to face Grandmother Greenslade's enthusiastic account—repeated several times—of her luncheon with him. Benjamin and Penny were doing their homework; Sophy sat curled up in the roomy armchair by the fire, with the Blot on her feet, and Titus on her lap, and a calm serenity on her nice face which showed nothing of the unhappy state of her mind. Mrs Greenslade paused in her highly colourful description of the Soufflé Rothschild she had enjoyed, and asked,

'Are you all right, darling? Tired or something?' She didn't wait for a reply, but added, 'I almost forgot, Uncle Giles telephoned. Just to see how we were, you know. He says he feels better already. He wanted to know if you were looking after Max.' She broke off and sent an enquiring look across the room to her granddaughter, who returned it calmly, and said,

'Granny, Max is well able to look after himself, and he wouldn't take any notice of me anyway, so let's not pretend that he would.' And to forestall the questions she could see her grandmother was about to launch at her, she embarked on an account of Mary's attempts to attract the Dutchman; leaving out the bit when he had said that he wasn't available.

Grandmother Greenslade laughed gently, and gave it as her opinion that Mary had been wasting her time. 'I fancy that Max is the type of man to prefer a girl less obvious than Mary,' she said rather dryly. 'I rather gathered that he doesn't lack companionship if he chooses to spend an evening in town.'

Sophy stirred, so that Titus was forced to put out a sleepy paw and anchor himself more firmly. 'Tell me some more about the clothes you saw at Wilton's,' asked Sophy. Somehow she hadn't wanted to hear any more about Max and his evenings out.

She spent her days off catching up on the ever-recurring chores, and went back on Friday singularly unrefreshed, but determined on at least one thing; that no one—and certainly not Max—must ever know how she felt about him. He would be gone in a few weeks, she had argued with herself. 'Out of sight, out of mind,' she had reminded herself, with a total lack of conviction.

The ear, nose and throat theatre was temporarily out of service, and the morning was to be given up to Mr Cass, the ENT specialist. Sophy spent a busy few hours handing sponges and guillotines and curettes to be used on a succession of small unconscious cherubs, who would presently regain consciousness in the Children's Unit, and rage defiance and temper at the patient nurses, until solaced with ice-cream.

It was a scramble to get ready in time for the afternoon list. Nurse Winters had days off, and although Robins was doing her best, she slowed them up quite a bit. They were to start at half past one. At a quarter past, Sophy told Staff to scrub for the first case, and herself went down for a quick dinner. The case, a second stage skin graft, was just leaving theatre as she went in, ready scrubbed and gowned. Max, standing by the table, pulling off his gloves, gave her a long stare, and nodded briefly in answer to her composed good afternoon. She went over to her trolleys and checked that there was nothing forgotten; Staff was already dishing for the following case. The afternoon passed quickly; she watched Max do a thyroidectomy, an amputation of foot, and a mastectomy with relaxed perfection and a complete lack of tiredness, not shared by his companions who, by five o'clock, were longing for a cup of tea. Sophy sent the nurses, one by one, for their own teas, and thought hopefully that he might call a halt before the last case, but he stood aside, watching them down his long nose while they prepared once more with speedy care, and the theatre porters adjusted the table.

The moment the men had left the theatre, Robins disappeared into the cubbyhole, to appear a minute later with the words, 'I've made you some tea, Sister.' Sophy beamed at her, divested herself of her gown and went and sat in the peaceful stuffiness, with her shoes kicked off and her theatre cap pushed anyhow to the back of her head. The tea was delicious: hot and strong and milky. She took a reviving gulp and choked on it. Max van Oosterwelde was standing in the little archway between the cubbyhole and the corridor. She put her cup down, still spluttering, and used her feet in a wild search for her shoes. He said on a gentle enquiring note,

'Did I startle you? No, never mind your shoes. Tom Carruthers has just told me that you have been working all day with only a very short dinner break. I blame myself that I did not think of it; we could have stopped for ten minutes during the afternoon. I am afraid that I forget everything but my work when I am operating. I'm going down to the wards now; I'll be outside in about twenty minutes, I'll give you a lift home.'

Sophy was aware of a little spark of temper flickering under her tiredness. She put down her cup, smiled at him, and said quietly, 'How kind. But I'm not in the least tired. I shall enjoy the walk.'

'*Cum grano salis*,' he murmured.

Sophy frowned. 'Eh?' she asked, with a complete lack of manners. 'Oh, Latin.' She pondered, and then said rather crossly, 'Well, I am tired.' Her look was apologetic. 'It was silly to fib about it.'

'Yes, it was,' he agreed equably, and went away. The comfort of the big car was almost overwhelming; she sat silent while it wove its way through the sudden spate of evening traffic, carefully not looking at the man beside her: It was easier to be casual that way. Even so, her heart gave its now familiar leap when he spoke.

'Going out tonight, Sophy?'

A little devil inside Sophy answered before she could stop it. 'Yes, I am,' she replied airily. 'To the cinema and supper afterwards.'

'And now he rears his ugly head,' Max said softly.

Sophy allowed herself a brief glimpse, and asked, puzzled, 'Whose head?'

'Why, the boy-friend's. Who else?'

Sophy caught her breath. Her honest nature urged her to confess at once and make a joke of it, but the little devil thought otherwise. 'He's not ugly,' she said. 'He's good-looking...and tall. Not too tall,' she added hastily.

Max stopped the car outside her door. 'Black wavy hair and blue eyes?' he enquired.

Sophy had the bit between her teeth. She turned wide eyes on to the man beside her, and flicked her eyelashes devastatingly. 'How did you know?' she asked, and greatly daring. 'Have you met him?'

Max savoured the eyelashes and answered slowly, 'No, I think not—I don't know his name, do I?'

'John Austin,' she said quickly.

'What's his job?' He sounded very casual.

Sophy thought quickly. Not a doctor; that would be too risky. 'He's a bank manager. In the City,' she elaborated.

The black brows lifted very slightly. 'Very nice

too.' Max said pleasantly. 'Well, I won't keep you, or you'll miss that film.'

He opened her door, and she got out and went quickly indoors, to stand against the front door, wondering just what she had started.

There was no regular theatre list on Saturday, but more often than not the weekly big clean was interrupted by emergencies. There was just such an emergency during the morning. Max van Oosterwelde, with Bill Evans at his heels, arrived quietly; skilfully went to work on the crushed body, sent it back to the Intensive Care Unit, and disappeared again.

There was an appendix in the afternoon—a perforation. Max worked steadily, giving Bill a good deal to do, and encouraging him as he did it. Sophy, standing small and straight on her platform behind the trolleys, allowed herself the pleasure of watching Max as he worked. He looked up suddenly, and caught her staring.

'Was the film good?' he asked idly.

'Yes, very.' She wasn't lying. Penny had seen it; she was merely passing on what she had said. He nodded, and turned away with the air of a man who had done his duty conversation-wise, and became involved in a highly technical argument with Dr Walters and Bill; it concerned car engines, and effectively excluded her, for she had no idea what went on under a car's bonnet.

Despite the necessary interruptions, she got away punctually, leaving Staff with one nurse for company and the rest of an instrument cupboard to turn out.

She was so surprised to see Max on the steps that she stopped short.

'Going home?' he asked smoothly. 'I'll drop you—you don't want to keep the boy-friend waiting.'

Sophy had forgotten all about that mythical gentleman; it was only when she was seated in the car that she replied belatedly, 'He's gone home for the weekend.'

Max switched on the engine and allowed it to idle and leaned back comfortably; obviously he had all the time in the world.

'Doesn't he live in London?'

'Yes, but his family live in—in Harrogate.' It was the first town that entered her head.

Jonkheer van Oosterwelde's brows lifted and the merest suspicion of a twitch appeared at the corner of his mouth; to be instantly suppressed.

'That's quite a trip. Still, if he had a good car...' He left the remark in mid-air. Sophy, brooding over the type of car a bank manager might be supposed to own, was relieved when he continued, 'I've tickets for the theatre. The—er—friend I was taking has had to cry off with a heavy cold. It seems a pity to waste them: I wonder if you would care to give me the pleasure of your company?'

Sophy's heart leapt; for a fraction of a second her face was alight with pleasure and excitement, then the clean sponge of her common sense wiped the delight from her face, and she answered soberly, 'Thank you for asking me, but I don't think...' She was interrupted.

'Ah, he might not like it. Is that it?' Max looked sideways at her with a hint of mockery which made

her blush. 'I assure you that he has no need to be
uneasy…I'm almost old enough to be your father, and
as I pointed out to you, I have no desire to flirt with
you.' He watched the blush re-kindle in her cheeks.
'Let me have his telephone number, and I'll give him
a ring, if that will make you happier.'

Sophy could conceive of nothing less likely to
make her happy. 'All the way to Harrogate?' she
asked faintly.

He was surprised. 'Why not? That's what tele-
phones are for.' He already had a slim pocket book
in his hand, and pen poised.

Sophy managed what she hoped sounded like a
light laugh. 'There's really no need for that. I should
like to come very much.' She was unaware of her
almost comical look of relief as he put the book away
again, and said,

'Good. I'll call for you about six-thirty. We'll dine
first, shall we?'

The short journey was finished in silence, but as
they drew up to the house, he leaned over to open the
door for her and said,

'Would Claridges suit you? And perhaps after the
show we might dance for a little while.'

Sophy thought that for someone as deceitful as she
had been, the punishment hardly fitted the crime; it
promised to be a delightful evening. That gloomy old
proverb 'Be sure your sins will find you out' stalked
fierily before her eyes. She gave it a metaphorical
kick. She smiled at him, and suddenly looked very
pretty.

'It sounds simply gorgeous,' said Sophy, and

jumped out of the car. She swung round. 'But how can we? You're on call.'

'No, I'm not. Tom Carruthers is taking over for me until tomorrow morning.'

He waved a careless hand, and the Bentley shot away in a powerful silence.

When she came downstairs, almost an hour later, Max was waiting in the hall. Penny and Benjamin were with him, and at the faint rustle of her dress they stopped talking and looked up at her. She had chosen to wear the amber Thai silk; it had a low scooped-out neckline and tiny sleeves, and fell, swirling to her neat ankles. It had a ridiculous neat waist, which showed off her pretty figure to perfection. She had taken great pains with her face and her mousy hair shone with subdued light from its vigorous brushing. She had her mother's squirrel coat over one arm; she hoped that Claridges and Max—above all, Max— would approve of her. He left the others and crossed the hall to meet her. He was wearing a dinner jacket and looked...she searched for a word...magnificent. She smiled shyly and said rather breathlessly,

'I must say goodnight to Grandmother.'

He took her coat and put it over his own arm. 'You look charming, Sophy,' he said, and gave her a little bow. 'May I come and say goodnight too?'

They were escorted to the door by the whole family, and that meant Sinclair and the Blot and Titus, who had to be discouraged from toadying to Max's well-polished shoes. There was a lot of talk and laughter, which was perhaps why Sophy sat so quiet and thoughtful as Max drove the Bentley through the streets.

'Are you sorry you came?' he enquired.

'No, of course not; only I don't get out often… I…I might be rather a dull companion.'

She had quite forgotten John Austin, and her companion, for some reason best known to himself, didn't choose to remind her.

'I haven't found you dull yet; while I am operating, my work is considerably enlivened by you.'

Sophy frowned, she had striven to become a perfect theatre sister. 'Do you find me amusing?' she asked in a cool voice.

'No, but you are a delight to watch. There is nothing to be seen of you but eyes and eyebrows, and it seems to me that you control the entire theatre with either the one or the other, and occasionally both. Only in moments of great urgency have I seen you raise a hand or snap the Cheatles above your head.'

'How can you possibly see all that when you're operating?' asked Sophy.

He shrugged. 'Surely you too have one small corner of your mind free while you work, where your thoughts are unimpeded?'

Sophy blushed faintly, remembering that any spare thoughts she had in theatre were of him. Fortunately there was no need for her to reply, for they had arrived at Claridges.

Their table was a good one, and she noted without surprise that Max was obviously known to the staff; the fact made him seem more remote than ever. She looked up from a menu which read like a gourmet's dream, and met the cool gaze that could so disconcert her.

'You looked sad. Why?'

Sophy shook her head and laughed a little, but said nothing, and he didn't repeat his question, but turned to his own menu.

'I hope you're hungry.' He glanced at the thin gold watch on his wrist. 'We don't need to hurry. What would you like?'

Sophy took another look and said with her usual good sense, 'I should like you to choose, please; I don't know enough about it.'

He gave her an approving look, and she sat quiet while he conferred with the waiter. This done, he smiled at her and said, 'Would you rather be surprised, or shall I tell you what we are going to eat?'

'Tell me, please,' said Sophy, 'then I can anticipate everything with pleasure.'

'All right. Smoked Salmon Muscovite, then Tournedos Benjamin...'

Sophy gave a delighted chuckle. 'That should be delicious,' she said. 'How clever of you to choose it.'

His eyes twinkled. 'I couldn't resist it, I'm afraid. We'll have a cold Charlotte for a sweet. It's called Metternich—there isn't one called Sophy, though I daresay if I asked they would produce one for you.' He turned away to the important task of discussing the wine list, and Sophy sat idly watching him, wondering how she could have ever thought him too self-assured and arrogant; she was discovering how witty and amusing he could be.

Dinner was a success, so was the show afterwards,

and when Max suggested that they should go somewhere to dance, Sophy agreed happily.

He took her to a night-club by the river, where they
had a candlelit table overlooking the river, and Sophy
drank champagne and watched the moon come from
behind the clouds to cast pale light on the water. After
a while, they danced. Sophy had thought that they
might not suit; Max was so much taller than she was.
She discovered with an agreeable surprise that it
didn't seem to matter at all. They danced on and on,
never at a loss for something to say to each other.
She was seeing a side of him she had not guessed
at—the side, she thought shrewdly, that he seldom
showed. Probably on Monday he would barely notice
her.

It was after two o'clock when she said, 'I'm having
a wonderful time, but I think I should go home.'

He agreed at once. 'But one more dance first, don't
you think?'

She made no demur; indeed, she felt a small glow
of satisfaction that he was enjoying himself too.

They said very little as he drove her home through
the almost empty streets—the journey was almost
over when she said,

'I have to look at the number-plate of your car.'

'By all means. May I ask why?'

'Well, I don't have to see it really,' Sophy conceded. 'Perhaps you would tell me. Benjamin said I
should have noticed by now, but I forgot...'

He obligingly told her.

'Your initials,' she did some mental arithmetic,
'and the year you were born.' She gave a chortle of

pleasure. 'How lucky you were to...no, it wasn't luck, was it?'

He laughed and said apologetically, 'I'm afraid not, nor can I take any of the credit for finding it—I merely paid someone else to do so.'

Sophy's reflection that it must be pleasant to have sufficient money to indulge in whims of this sort was cut short by their arrival. He got out of the car and went to the door with her; and took the key and unlocked it. The hall looked cosy; barely lighted by a small wall lamp. Sophy wondered if she should ask him in, and to his secret amusement decided against it, offering a small, capable hand instead.

'I've had a delightful evening. Thank you very much.' She hesitated. 'I hope your friend gets over her cold quickly.' She couldn't see her companion's face very clearly, but she had the odd feeling that he was laughing.

He released her hand, and said, 'As I hope John—er—Austin had a speedy return from...where was it?... Harrogate. Goodnight.'

He held the door open for her, and she slipped through, and he closed it behind her. She switched off the little lamp, and went upstairs to bed through the well-remembered dark of her home, with the troublesome presence of Mr Austin stalking beside her.

Despite the fact that Sophy went to church, cooked the Sunday dinner, took the Blot for a long walk which neither of them really enjoyed, and wrote a number of unnecessary letters, she had far too much time to think about Max. The family had listened enthralled to her account of the previous evening's delights, but she could not talk about them to the exclusion of everything else.

She was glad when it was Monday again. There was a long, exacting list in theatre; probably Max would have nothing to say to her beyond a civil good morning, but at least she would see him. She almost ran to the hospital in her anxiety to be under the same roof as he was, quite forgetful of her resolve not to see more of him than was necessary for their work. But this didn't matter, anyway; Max was friendly and pleasant, but evinced no desire for her company. Indeed, he spent several hours with Penny and Benjamin and Grandmother Greenslade, and stayed to tea, on the one day in the week when she was on duty from eleven until eight in the evening. She told herself that she didn't mind in the least, and was very careful, when she saw him next, to let him see that she hadn't minded at all.

Sunday came round once more. Staff had the weekend off, so had Winters. That left Vincent, the third-year nurse, and Robins, and both theatre porters on duty. It seemed a crowd, but one of the porters and Vincent had half days. The day passed uneventfully and she filled it with the hundred and one small jobs which had accumulated during the week. Tom Carruthers came up and they went over the next week's list together while they had their coffee, and he had then gone away again to read the Sunday papers. It was about five o'clock when two RTAs arrived together, and Sophy, answering a cry for help from Cas sent the remaining porter down to help out. Robins was painstakingly folding masks, and Sophy went

back to her lists and requisitions, to be interrupted
shortly by Tom on the telephone.

'We've got six nasty ones down here. We'll have
to do one as soon as we can get some blood into him.
Can you manage forty minutes, Sophy? Pelvic crush
and very dicey.' He didn't wait for an answer, for he
knew that Sophy would be ready—she always was.
'Sophy? Can you spare your man for a bit longer?
It's all hell let loose down here.' Sophy said Yes, for
there was nothing else to say, and hung up, and went
into the theatre. She looked at Robins and wished
fleetingly that she had someone else on duty, then
dismissed the thought as a waste of time. Robins was
still slow and nervous, but she knew the routine now,
and Sophy set her to work, while she herself put up
the Lloyd-Davies crutches and the stirrups—the patient would almost certainly be put in Trendelenberg-
lithotomy position. She put the extra instruments they
would need into the second autoclave, and presently,
gowned and masked and gloved, she laid up the theatre, her small sterile person whisking around with
methodical, precise speed.

She was arranging knives and forceps on the
Mayo's table when she heard the gentle swish of the
trolley's rubber tyres, and then the murmur of voices
from the anaesthetic room. Her sharp ears heard the
sound of running water in the scrub room too, and
she nodded to Robins to go there, ready to tie the
gowns as the surgeons were ready.

She was taken by surprise when Max sauntered in
and took up a position well away from the table,
where they were busy arranging the patient. Her heart
bounced against her ribs, and her voice, in answer to

his civil good evening, was a shaky squeak. But by the time the two men were standing each side of the patient she had command of herself once more, and was able to reply in her usual pleasant, level voice when Max looked around the theatre and asked if the nurses had gone on strike.

'It's Sunday, sir,' she said sapiently, 'so only two nurses on after six o'clock. I've a porter too, but he's gone back to Cas to help out.' As she stopped speaking, an ambulance, its see-saw warning blaring urgently, went past in the street below.

Max dropped some discarded Spencer-Wells forceps on to the Mayo table. 'It sounds as though he will be very welcome there.' He shot a look across the theatre at Nurse Robins, whose eyes were glued on Sophy; her anxiety not to miss anything gave her the air of a long-distance runner the second before the starting pistol goes off. Sophy knew exactly what he was thinking, and said stoutly,

'Nurse Robins and I can manage perfectly well, sir.'

He had made a right paramedian incision, and he and Bill were busy tying off; he said crisply, without looking up, 'I have no doubt of that, Sister.'

They worked in silence for some time until Max said, 'Now let us assess the damage...'

The list was a formidable one involving a great deal of cutting out and patching up and sewing and stitching together.

'I'm surprised,' Max said, 'that an iron girder left us anything to work on.' He went on briskly. 'Right nephrectomy—I'll do it through this incision—repair of liver; suture of bladder, splenectomy and resection of gut. All right, Sister?'

'Quite all right, sir.'

Her voice sounded very faintly smug as she took a sterile towel from the end of one of trolleys, revealing all the extra instruments he would be likely to use. He took her foresight for granted, however, and she felt keen disappointment, instantly swallowed up by the necessity of paying close attention to her work.

An hour, an hour and a half went by unnoticed, while the crushed body on the table was slowly and methodically set to rights. Mostly there was a relaxed silence, broken from time to time by casual conversation. Sophy noted with satisfaction that the tension had gone out of Nurse Robins; due to the Dutchman, who had gone out of his way to joke gently with her and put her at her ease. Sophy eased her weight from one neatly shod foot to the other and then stiffened suddenly as the quiet of the theatre was shattered by the banshee wail of the fire alarm. Max took no notice of it whatever, and Bill, after a glance at his chief, ignored it too. Dr Walters twiddled a knob or two on the Boyle's machine and muttered, 'That's all we need.'

The alarm went on and on, searing the eardrums of its hearers. When it at length stopped, Max asked, 'Fire, Sister?' He didn't look up from his sewing.

Sophy, who was beginning to wonder if he had heard the hellish noise, put a Paul's tube and a glass rod on to the Mayo's table, and said dryly. 'I imagine so, sir. Nurse shall find out.'

She arched her eyebrows at Robins, who hurried over to her, missing the surgeon by such a narrow margin that Sophy's quick, indrawn breath sounded loud in the silence. She spoke in her usual measured tones, however, and Robins with an apprehensive glance at Max, slipped away.

He said, without looking up, 'Never mind, Sister. A miss is as good as a mile.'

She was saved from replying by the thunderous din of the fire engines taking the corner below in an accumulation of sound that made speech a useless thing. Robins, returning precipitately, had to wait, standing in an anguished silence until the last of them had wailed to a halt.

'Pratt says there's been an explosion in Edward—it's being evacuated, some patients and nurses are hurt. Alexander is being evacuated too—and Cas.'

Sophy stared at her, blinked, and said, 'Thank you, Nurse. We had better check swabs, hadn't we?'

She watched Robins start, then turned and started her own count. It didn't take her long; she stood patiently, waiting for the nurse to finish, her thoughts racing. The theatre suite was the corner stone between Centre Block and Edward and Alexander Cas was directly below. A door at the end of the theatre led to a landing containing a staircase and lift, which gave access to the wards and Casualty. She glanced instinctively towards the door—it was a nice solid one, she noticed with satisfaction, and there was the landing between...

Another fire engine sped past, and above its diminishing noise she heard the telephone ringing. Robins disappeared for a second time, and Sophy picked up a probe with her Cheatles and put it unerringly into the gloved hand hovering in front of her. Mechanically she gave Bill more swabs, rinsed a few instruments; took the loop off the diathermy handle and substituted a disc in obedience to Max's quiet order. The operation was going very well, but was by no means over. There was a good deal of noise by now, but it was muffled and she had neither the time nor the inclination to interpret it. Robins came back, almost running. Sophy said steadily in a warning voice, 'Don't come any nearer the table, Nurse, and please give us your message.' She watched the girl pull herself together, and said, 'Good girl! We're quite safe here, you know, for a long while yet.' She wished she could believe herself, but she sounded convincing, anyway.

'That was Matron, Sister. She says could Mr van Oosterwelde arrange to evacuate the theatre within ten minutes. They're trying to hold the fire in check, but the wind is blowing towards us…' She stopped, then said rather wildly, 'Oh, Sister, whatever shall we do?'

Sophy, resisting a desire to pass the question on to Max van Oosterwelde, said bracingly, 'Was that all the message, Nurse?'

Robins gulped. 'Matron asked if you needed help, because if you could manage she would be glad, as there isn't anyone to spare at the moment. And would you send the patient to George; they've turned one of their bathrooms into an intensive care unit.'

Sophy was amazed to hear Max laugh, and after a moment the other two men joined in. Evidently they saw humour in the situation; she frowned blackly at Bill, who stopped laughing long enough to explain that the idea of wheeling the patient in his present very unfinished state into one of old Mother Forbes' spotless bathrooms was just about the funniest thing that had happened for weeks. Sophy had to smile a little at that; Sister Forbes had a passion for an apple-pie order—she must be suffering acutely from an influx of patients who weren't hers and were probably too scared to care if they were disorganising her tidy ward.

Having deliberately eased the tension around him, Max said coolly, 'Telephone Matron and give her this message, please, Nurse. I regret that the theatre cannot be cleared for another hour; perhaps a little less than that. I should suggest that a couple of firemen come up and clear the anaesthetic room, don't you agree, Sister?'

Sophy wiped the stitch scissors carefully. 'A very good idea, sir,' she said cheerfully. At the moment at any rate, she found herself quite unable to feel even faintly frightened; she trusted Max completely, she had no need to worry.

Robins went away again, and Sophy took the opportunity to ask if it wouldn't be a good idea for the girl to stay in the anaesthetic room and help the firemen. 'Then they won't overlook anything,' she explained carefully, 'and it will keep Nurse busy.'

'Can you manage on your own?'

'Oh, yes. Nurse can stock me up before she goes, and I've got everything here that you could possibly need.'

He shot her a sharp glance. 'Very well, if that suits you, Sister.'

Nothing much happened—there was noise, naturally, but it seemed subdued and far away. Robins returned, did as she was bid, and disappeared yet again. They could hear subdued voices and the sounds made by people in a hurry trying to be quiet, coming from the anaesthetic room. A small pool of water had formed inside the door leading to Edward wing; obviously the firemen were somewhere, probably on the landing, using their hoses. Sophy still felt quite safe. When Robins came back, they checked swabs again before she set her to renew all the lotion bowls. The powerful lamp over the table went out without so much as a flicker to warn them. Max said something explosive as Sophy said, 'Emergency lights, Nurse. As quick as you can.' It was only seconds before they had light again, albeit one that had to be manoeuvred into exactly the right position. Sophy sent up a little prayer of thankfulness that she had had it overhauled within the last day or so. She tidied the Mayo's table, gave Bill some forceps and a further supply of swabs, then looked automatically around the theatre. The pool by the door had increased she noted, and blinked and looked again. A little wreath of smoke, dainty as grey chiffon was oozing round the door. Robins saw it too, and said before she could stop herself, 'Sister, the smoke's coming in.'

Sophy, forced to a normality she was no longer feeling observed, 'Yes, Nurse, so I see. There's bound to be a few stray wisps...the wind, you know.'

As if to give the lie to this erroneous remark, a framework of feathery black smoke erupted around the door, pushed from behind by some giant force. Sophy felt a prickle of sweat on her forehead, while icy fingers played a scale down her spine. With hands that shook only very slightly she wrung out several towels in water and piled them neatly where she could

snatch them up at speed, then gave a very wet one to
Robins with instructions to dampen the surgeons'
masks and then Dr Walker's, and to take a second
one with her Cheatles and lay it close to the patient's
face. The smoky frame doubled its size and a little of
it eddied away from the door. Max van Oosterwelde
straightened up from his stitching, put his discarded
needle holder down, and took the length of gut Sophy
was holding out between rigidly held hands. He said
quietly,

'You and Nurse go now, Sister, we can manage
very nicely now, I think.'

Sophy nodded to Robins, who came near enough
to whisper, 'You'll come too, Sister?'

Sophy didn't answer her question, but said softly,
so that Max wouldn't be able to hear, 'Report to Matron if you can find her—if not, anyone who ought to
know—police or firemen or someone like that—then
go to George and tell Sister you've come to help until
we bring the patient.' She winked cheerfully and
cocked her head towards the door. Robins rather uncertainly winked back, and slid quietly away.

Sophy threaded two needles; she thought she had
better do them while her hands were still under her
control. She jumped visibly when Max said gently.
'You too, Sister. I'm sure Bill can thread needles, and
I believe that I am still capable of picking up any
instruments I may need.'

The theatre was suddenly filled with sound—a
long-drawn-out, slow-motion noise of bricks and
girders and glass tumbling lazily. Max tied an artery
and Bill took off the forceps neatly, remarking cheerfully, 'Something's fallen down.'

'Edward's roof,' said Max, and tied off another artery. 'You will go now, Sister. I don't intend to tell
you again.'

Sophy drew a deep steadying breath. 'That's a
good thing, for I'm not going; not until this case is
finished.' She added 'Sir' as an afterthought. She
sounded tart.

He was intent on his work. 'Unfortunately I am not
in a position to enforce my order, Sister,' and then,
pleasantly, 'What a sharp-tongued little vixen you
are!'

Sophy snorted and busied herself piling discarded
instruments into one of the lotion bowls, with a vague
notion that she would be able to get them out of the
theatre later on. It was the sight of a thin, fitful line
of flames mingling with the smoke which caused her
to drop the instruments in her hand with a loud clatter.

'Regretting your disobedience, Sophy?' inquired
Max silkily. He held out his needle holder and she
inserted a curved needle into it.

'If you mean, am I frightened—yes, of course I am,
but I shan't faint or anything like that, you know.'

Max didn't answer this remark, but turned to Dr
Walters. 'I need another ten minutes—will he be all
right if you get that machine of yours out of the way,
do you think? He's well relaxed, I've got the muscle
sheath to stitch—I'll put in mattress stitches and we
can put clips on later.'

Dr Walters twiddled his knobs, nodded, and dis-
connected the machine. He slipped an airway into the
patient's mouth, and then, moving fast for once, disappeared with the Boyle's. He was back within seconds.

'Corridor's full of firemen and police and so forth,' he reported casually. 'Waiting to hose us down if need be, I suppose.'

He bent over his patient, and the door leading to what had been Edward Block fell into the theatre with a noise like a gigantic nut being cracked, and smoke and flames hurried in after it. The flames, halted by tiled walls and stone floor, hung back, but the smoke crept unhurriedly forward. Max tied the last careful knot with no apparent haste, and took the straight needle and thick gut Sophy was holding out in a frankly trembling hand. The incision was a long one; it would need at least five of the deep double stitches to hold it securely until such time as the clips could be put on. The flames had found a foothold on the wooden shelves used for the dressings, and had reached merrily for the ceiling with long eager tongues. Max held the gut of the last stitch for Bill to cut, and threw the needle on to a trolley. 'Start pumping, Bill.' The younger man put his foot on the lever which would make it possible for them to push the table across the theatre, and Max piled on gauze and a thick pad of wool Sophy had ready. She pushed her trolleys aside and flung several towels on top of the wool and topped them with a very damp one. They were ready to go when Max said urgently, 'Wait!'

The ceiling at the far end of the theatre was cracking, making little cheerful popping sounds; the cracks ran like threads pulled by invisible urgent fingers above the stretch of floor they must cross.

Sophy stood with a small hand on the patient's covered feet, drawing comfort from the human contact. When Max said, 'Come here, Sophy, to me,' she

obeyed gladly. He had an arm in a protective arc over
his patient, he drew her with the other one close
against him, and as she felt it tighten around her she
felt quite safe. She hadn't realised that she was shaking until he said, 'You're quivering like a jelly, Sophy. We're going to run for the door as soon as we
know if the ceiling is going to hold or no. When I
say so, steady the patient. We'll do the pushing,' They
reached the door as the ceiling around the burning
door caved in, and smoke and flames poured into the
theatre. The corridor was packed with firemen and
hoses and police and ambulance men. There was no
lack of help; within seconds the patient was transferred on to a trolley, covered in blankets, and was
being piloted through the throng by two police con-
stables. Centre Block corridor was like Hammersmith
Broadway on a Saturday afternoon; nurses pushing
old gentlemen in wheelchairs; ambulance men carrying blankets, small children or old ladies; a group
of earnest housemen applying heart massage to a patient who had come in for rest and quiet…even the
Assistant Matron, looking harassed, struggling along
with a waste paper basket full of bottles of pills and
medicine. The whole set-up was so unusual that when
Staff, unrecognisable in a trouser suit and a rather
overpowering fox fur hat, joined their cortège, Sophy
accepted her arrival without so much as a lift of the
eyebrows, merely asking her in a matter-of-fact sort
of voice if she would mind going to Orthopaedic Theatre to borrow the Michel clips holder and clips and
some gloves and dressing packs.

Sister Forbes came to meet them as they battled
their way through George, metaphorically wringing

her hands—her erstwhile pristine ward looked like
Clapham Junction on a Bank Holiday. The illusion
was heightened by the dispensing of tea by an enthusiastic posse led by the ward orderlies. Sophy saw two
boys in running shorts, a priest, an elderly woman,
obviously straight from church, for she still clutched
her prayer book, and a retired gentleman in a bowler
hat. Sophy suppressed a giggle, as Sister Forbes,
stalking along beside them, expressed her view of
people who moved in on her ward without so much
as a by-your-leave. She avoided Bill's eye, and listened in something like awe to Max, who, with exactly the right mixture of charm and authority, had
Sister Forbes a willing disciple by the time they
reached the bathroom, so that the operation was completed with the maximum of sterility and the minimum of delay. There was even a staff nurse to take
over the nursing of the patient, so that Sophy was able
to go back to the theatre wing, accompanied by Staff,
willing, but very hot in the fur hat. The corridor was
a shambles, but the fire had been contained in the
theatre itself. The lotion bowls, loaded down with instruments, had been saved, so had a glass cupboard,
the glass splintered all over its contents. Sophy
changed her gown, Cooper removed her jacket and
the hat, and tied herself into a gown too, and the pair
of them retired to her office, where there was a small
basin. There was a great deal of activity still, but no
one had told them to go; Sophy collected a great
many towels from the cupboard in the corridor, and
they set to work. The light from the emergency lamp
was dim, but better than total darkness; they were
making good headway when there was a timid knock

on the door and Robins came in. Sophy tossed her a towel.

'Nurse Robins did very well,' she told Staff. 'She's going to make a good nurse one day.'

She was rewarded by a beaming smile. 'You didn't mind me coming back, Sister? There's heaps of staff on now—all the part-timers seem to be here. I thought there might be something to do. Is it safe?' she asked in a carefully casual voice.

Sophy shrugged. 'I don't know; but I think it must be. No one stopped us, and I can't see any fire damage in the corridor.'

They had done the used instruments and laid them in neat heaps on a clean towel, and were about to clear the cupboard outside when Matron walked in. Save for her cap—which was askew—she might have been making her daily ceremonial round.

'I should like to borrow your nurses, Sister Greenslade—they're badly needed for escort duties on the ambulances.'

Her eyes rested momentarily on Staff Nurse Cooper's purple trousered legs, emerging from beneath her theatre gown. 'You came back from your day off, Staff Nurse? How good of you—I wonder if you would spare an hour?' She watched the two girls speed away, and turned to Sophy.

'And you, Sister—could you give a hand in Casualty? I'm afraid some of the staff were injured, and they are hard pressed. You'll find them in the Board Room.'

It was crowded—Sophy stood for a moment, getting her bearings—there were patients on trolleys, mattresses and chairs. There were a couple of sterilisers bubbling away in one corner, and a great pile of dressing packets on the Board Room table, which had been pushed to one side. There seemed to be a great many housemen there, and quite a lot of nurses. She was accosted almost at once by the staff nurse on Cas, who said,

'Oh, Sister. Have you come to take over? We're not a bit organised...'

'Where's Sister?' asked Sophy.

'She was injured—not badly, luckily—but she'll be off for a day or so.' She looked hopefully at Sophy.

It took quite a few minutes to get the housemen sorted into teams with the nurses, and even longer to make sure that everyone had a fair share of what instruments there were. Sophie hadn't seen Max arrive; she turned from the steaming sterilisers to find him at her elbow. She felt a momentary flash of vexation that he had to come and see her like this—straggly hair, a damp flushed face—his faintly amused look made her very aware of her appearance. He made it worse by saying,

'How now, you secret, black and midnight hag... What is't you do?'

Sophy frowned heavily; did he really expect her to remember her Shakespeare at such a time? It just so happened she remembered what came next. 'A deed without a name,' she said crossly.

He was helping himself to instruments. 'Let the charmed pot boil on its own. I need you over by the door—bring some dressings with you.'

There was a fireman lying propped up against the wall just inside the door. His eyes were closed and his face was ashen; one sleeve of his jacket was soaked with blood. Sophy dropped on her knees and started to cut the sleeve open.

'I found him in Casualty,' said Max. 'He's lost quite a lot of blood, I fancy. I'll stop the haemorrhage and get him off to St Chad's as quickly as possible.'

There was a deep gash running from the man's wrist to above the elbow; Sophy held the arm up while Max put on a tourniquet, then started to clean up the mess. It took a little while to find the severed ends of the artery and tie it off. There was no point in closing the wound; the tendons were severed too. Sophy loosened the tourniquet while Max applied antibiotic, and then he went to telephone St Chad's while she put on a temporary dressing. She had just finished when he came back.

'They'll take him. See that a nurse goes with him, will you, Sister?' He was away before she could speak. Sophy sighed, put a blanket over the man, and went to look for an ambulance. The patient was being loaded on to a stretcher when Night Super put her head round the door.

'There you are,' she said comfortably. 'Sister Fox will take over from you—and there are plenty of nurses to relieve this lot.' As she spoke Sister Fox, with a retinue of helpers, arrived. Within five minutes Sophy had given her some sort of a report, made sure that the nurses' changeover was completed, and, wrapped in a borrowed cloak took her place beside the fireman in the ambulance. It seemed much easier to go herself than take a nurse from duty, besides, she told herself, she wasn't tired. An hour later, coming out of St Chad's Casualty, she realised how mistaken she was. She pushed the swing doors open and started down the long corridor to Night Sister's office—the ambulance had gone long ago; she would have to get a lift. She yawned prodigiously, and tripped over the cloak she had hung over one shoulder.

Jonkheer van Oosterwelde stretched out a long arm and set her neatly back on to her feet again. 'There you are,' he said. 'I didn't mean you to go in the ambulance, you know,' he added mildly.

Sophy looked at him tiredly; she didn't mind any more how she looked. 'Everyone was going off duty,' she explained, 'and the nurses coming on were badly needed.' She yawned again. 'He's had a litre of blood and went to the theatre a few minutes ago.'

'You stayed to help, I gather,' he remarked dryly.

'Yes, they're awfully busy.' He made a little sound, and she asked, 'You came to see how he was?'

'No, I came to take you home.'

She stood still, looking at him with her beautiful eyes. 'How kind,' she said, 'but you needn't have bothered. I was going back on my broomstick.'

He laughed at that and caught her by the arm and hurried out to where the Bentley was waiting. It was cold and damp and inclined to fog. Sophy shivered.

'Hungry?' he asked.

Sophy realised that she was—very. She had no idea of the time; tea had obviously been hours ago. 'Famished,' she replied, and started making futile attempts to tidy her regrettable hair. Max had switched on the engine; he switched it off again, took a comb from a pocket and said 'Here, let me.' She sat quietly while he tucked and pinned the ends away under her cap. When he had finished, he put a finger under her chin and looked at her; his head on one side. Sophy looked back at him shyly, hearing her heartbeats pounding in her ears, and making an effort to take regular breaths; the effort wasn't very successful, and when he bent his head and kissed her gently on the mouth, she stopped breathing altogether; savouring bliss, but only for a moment. He let her go, and said with a soft laugh, 'You poor scrap, you're worn out, aren't you?'

Sophy sat up very straight; his pity hurt. She supposed that he would have kissed a fallen child in the same kindly, casual way. She felt cold and empty and shivered again.

'The sooner we find something to eat the better,' he said.

They didn't need to go far. The all-night coffee stall had several customers; they looked at Sophy and Max with some interest as they approached. Max pulled a box up to the side of the stall and told Sophy to sit down, then ordered tea and sandwiches with the same unconscious ease that he had used at Claridges. The stall owner filled two mugs and watched while Max handed Sophy hers.

'Bin in that 'ospital fire?' he asked. ''Ad someone 'ere jist now, said the operating theatre was burnt out. Everyone inside burnt to a crisp, he said.' He sliced bread and spread it with a lavish hand. 'Not prying, yer understand. But seeing as this young lady's an 'ospital Sister...'

Max took the sandwiches and gave them to Sophy. 'Yes, we were in the fire, but it's all out now, there's just the clearing up to do. And I can assure you that no one in the theatre was burned to a crisp.' Everyone looked at Sophy, contentedly munching; she was miserable, but she was hungry too; for the moment hunger triumphed. She smiled at the ring of faces, and they smiled back at her, and the cold misery inside her wasn't so bad any more. She had a second sandwich and another cup of tea, and listened to Max, completely at ease, joining in a discussion on boxing. She closed her eyes, and woke a minute later to find him bending over her. He said something she couldn't understand, but it sounded gentle, then he said briskly in English. 'What a thoughtless fool I am! Come on, girl. Home for you.'

She wished everyone a sleepy goodnight, and Max sent the Bentley purring along the quiet streets.

'Poor Uncle Giles.' She had just remembered him. 'What a shock it will be to him.'

'I'll telephone him first thing in the morning before he gets the papers. It may be a good thing, you know; the longer holiday he has, the better.'

He drew up before the house; there was a light on in the sitting room. Sophy saw it and said with a little gasp, 'Oh, I hope they haven't been worried.'

'I should have told you—I saw Ben just after we left George. I couldn't get to him, but Bill did; he will have told him that you were all right.'

He got out of the car and went to the door with her. Sinclair opened it. He put out a hand and said, 'Miss Sophy!' He swallowed, and tried again. 'You gave us a fright.'

Sophy flung her arms around him. 'Sinclair dear, I'm so sorry I didn't send a message or something. There wasn't time, you know.' She went past him into the hall. 'Are they all asleep?'

'The children are—I hope. Mrs Greenslade's dozing in the sitting room.' Sophy turned back to Max.

Before she could speak, he said, half-laughing, 'No, I won't come in. Go to bed, Sophy. You'll be needed in the morning.' He lifted a hand in salute, and went away. Sophy watched his broad back as he walked back to the car, and then looked rather blankly at Sinclair.

'I'll go and see Granny,' she said softly. 'Good-night, Sinclair.' She smiled at him, but she didn't really see him, only Max.

CHAPTER FIVE

THE NEXT DAY was a drudgery of hard work; there was naturally no theatre list. Sophy lent her nurses to the hard-pressed wards and spent a long day salvaging and drying out equipment, and counting the cost in lost instruments and dressings and all the specialised stock that had had to be left behind in the theatre. She was surprised that she could find anything at all; the theatre was an empty shell, with walls and floor intact but a ceiling open to the sky. She looked around with sober eyes, and decided that whatever the future held for her, she had plenty of work to get on with. She went into the cubbyhole to make a cup of tea, realised that there was no electricity and banged the kettle down in a sudden spurt of temper—the whole place was a ruin, and would take months to rebuild. It looked as though the hospital had a Theatre Sister without a job! She looked at the clock; it was barely ten, but she needed a cup of coffee. She rolled down her sleeves and found her cuffs, then started off for Orthopaedic. Mary would give her some; the list there didn't start until eleven o'clock. She was crossing the main entrance hall when she saw Max. He was talking to Mr Potts and Mr Gowan, two of the surgical consultants, and didn't see her. He looked tired; the lines of his face deeply etched; she thought that he had probably not been to bed. She looked away hurriedly and turned into Orthopaedic corridor, determinedly not thinking of the previous night—perhaps, she thought, he would seek her out later on in the day. Her thoughts went back unbidden however, and she remembered with a sick pang that he hadn't once asked her if she was all right—to be called a sharp-tongued vixen and a jelly and a poor scrap was hardly indicative of the sort of interest she seemed incapable of inspiring.

Mary was glad to see her and pressed coffee and biscuits and the best chair upon her guest.

'What happened?' she wanted to know, her blue eyes wide with curiosity. 'Your Nurse Robins told my Nurse Todd that van Oosterwelde told you to leave the theatre with her—but you didn't, did you? What happened, couldn't you get away in time?'

Sophy helped herself to another biscuit. 'Yes, of course I could. But they needed another pair of hands, if only to check swabs and find things; you know how men never see anything they're looking for.'

Mary nodded understandingly. 'Yes,' she remarked, 'they make a complicated incision no one would dare to attempt, and then can't find a needle to sew it together again. Was he nice?' she asked suddenly.

Sophy nodded. 'Yes—very. If he was scared it didn't show; he just went on working as though nothing was happening.'

She smiled at nothing and then went scarlet as Mary observed,

'You've fallen for him, haven't you, Sophy? Hard luck, my dear. You haven't a chance...I mean, look how he treated me'—she spoke with a genuine lack of conceit—'if I couldn't catch his eye, you certainly won't.'

Sophy put down her cup. 'He'll be going back to Holland very soon now, there's no work for him here, is there?' She tried to think of something clever to say and failed. 'Thanks for the coffee.'

There was no sign of Max as she went back to the theatre. Tom Carruthers came up during the afternoon. As he opened her office door she looked up, quite failing to hide her disappointment. He studied her thoughtfully and decided that she really was a plain girl after all—perhaps she was tired. He sat down opposite her and she looked at him and smiled, and he knew he'd been wrong—she wasn't plain at all. They talked about the fire for a little while. 'Have we lost an awful lot of stuff?' he wanted to know. She told him... 'And I've not finished yet. The theatre will need rebuilding—have you seen it?' They went together and peered at it from the safety of the doorway.

'Months of work,' he muttered. 'We're to have St Chad's theatre twice a week; they'll admit the patients and we'll have them back for post-operative treatment. What's happening to you?'

Sophy shrugged her shoulders. 'I don't know. Holiday Relief, I expect.' She made a face; no one liked the job—no two Sisters worked alike; you worked your way from ward to ward, leaving a trail of annoyed Sisters behind you...

They went back to her office and she opened the catalogue at the instrument section and began painstakingly checking her list with it. Tom leaned forward and took the catalogue from her. 'I'll call them out, you tick them; it'll be quicker.'

She gave him a grateful look, and for a little while they worked in a companionable silence. Half way through the page of catheters, he said, 'Have you seen van Oosterwelde today?'

Sophy stopped, her finger poised over a nice little illustration of Bozeman's two-way catheter. 'No,' she said carefully. 'Did—did he come up here?'

Carruthers kept his eyes on his list. 'No. He was up all night—he went for a bath and shave about nine. He's had some news from Utrecht, apparently the theatre at the hospital there is ready sooner than was expected. He'll be off shortly, I imagine...not much point in him staying, the way things are. I shall miss him, he's a very nice fellow.' He glanced quickly across the desk and then down again.

Sophy's face was bent over her work; she waited a minute until she was sure that her voice would sound normal. 'That will be splendid for him, won't it? We shall all miss him, but he never intended to stay, did he?' She didn't want to talk about him any more, because that would mean thinking about him as well, and she couldn't bear to do that. She said cheerfully, 'Uncle Giles telephoned this morning; he's upset, but he can't work anyway, so it's not too bad for him. He said he was feeling much better.' She didn't wait for Carruthers to reply, but went on without pause, 'Should I order all the gum-elastics, do you think?' She jumped up and fetched the Formalin vapour covered dish where they were kept. 'They must have got very hot, for they don't look quite...'

Tom looked at them. 'You're right, you'll need a new set. Throw those out.'

Sophy put them back carefully. 'Don't be silly—I have to show everything to someone or other before I can get it replaced.'

At half-past five, he threw down his work. 'We're off duty as from now. I've got seats for the theatre…' and he named the play.

She spoke before she thought. 'It's lovely!'

'Didn't know you'd seen it.' Tom looked vaguely surprised.

Sophy went very red, and said with an appalling honesty, 'I was invited in place of someone who couldn't go at the last minute.'

It was far worse when she got home. They waited until she was sitting comfortably in front of the fire, munching toast.

'Max came in just as we were sitting down to lunch.' It was Penny who spoke.

Sophy put down the finger of toast and clasped her hands on her lap, so that each should hold the other steady. She felt as though she had been turned to stone. This view was shared by the Blot, who was sitting next to her and experimentally extended a long pink tongue, wrapped it neatly around the toast, and swallowed it with a soundless gulp, his melting eyes on Sophy's face, on the alert for the reprimand he expected. None was forthcoming, although she had seen him doing it; with a perception stronger than that of the humans around him, he saw she wanted comfort. He extended his tongue once more, this time to give her hand a gentle lick.

'He's gone down to Dorset to see Uncle Giles,' her

grandmother interposed. She lifted her eyes briefly
from her crossword puzzle and smiled gently in Sophy's direction. 'He didn't stay long. He's going back
to Utrecht in a few days...but I expect you know all
about that.'

Sophy unclasped her hands, drank some tea, looked
at her empty plate and exchanged a long loving look
with the Blot, 'Tom Carruthers told me he would be
leaving soon,' she answered briefly. 'I didn't see him
myself.' She met her brother's enquiring eye. 'He was
up all night, and very busy this morning.'

Ben was not to be put off. 'Yes, but if he had time
to come and see us before he went, why didn't he go
and see you too? You were much nearer to him than
we were.'

Sophy scrambled to her feet and made a great deal
of work of clearing away her tea and giving Titus his
milk.

'I dare say he may have gone to the theatre while
I was away this morning. I had to go to Mary's for
coffee—there's no electricity in theatre block.' This
piece of information led, as she had hoped it would,
to talk of the fire, and Max wasn't mentioned again.

The next few days were very dull. She plodded on
steadily with her checking and listing; it was going
to take much longer than she had at first thought.
There were workmen in the theatre already, covering
the roof with tarpaulins, and clearing away the vast
amount of rubble. She saw little of her nurses, and
not very much of Tom or Bill Evans, although the
latter came to supper. Sophy went on duty each morning dreading to be met with the news that Max van
Oosterwelde had gone without saying goodbye. When

he did at last walk into her office, she was quite un-prepared for him—kneeling on the floor, surrounded by packets of needles, which she was sorting carefully into sizes and shapes. Colour flooded her face as she looked up and saw him standing in the doorway. She scrambled to her feet and said rather breathlessly,

'Hullo. How's…how's Uncle Giles?'

Max smiled faintly. 'Going along very nicely—and how is Sophy?'

'Me? I'm fine, thank you.'

'And since you have not enquired as to the state of my health, let me assure you at once that it is good.' He cocked his head to one side, and the cold after-noon sun turned his hair to silver. 'You look thinner, and white and tired.' he observed. 'Are you alone up here all day—', he waved a nicely kept hand—'clear-ing up this mess?'

'Well, yes. It's my job, isn't it?'

'And what will you do when you have found the last needle and counted the last dressing towel?'

'I don't know—I expect I'll have to do holiday relief; they don't want me at St Chad's, and the the-atre will take months to rebuild. I asked a man who came to look at it yesterday—an architect, I think.'

'You'll hate relief work, won't you?'

He went and sat on a corner of the desk, and it creaked under his weight. He was wearing tweeds and a polonecked sweater, and she supposed that he had come straight from Uncle Giles. He gave her a sharp look from blue eyes that seemed expressionless. 'I'm going back to Utrecht tomorrow evening,' he said slowly. 'I should have liked to ask you to spend another evening with me before I go. Unfortunately I'm not free tonight.'

Sophy dumped a pile of needle packets on to the desk, careless of the fact that they had been sorted once and would now have to be done again. 'That would have been delightful.' To her satisfaction her voice sounded just as she wanted it to; pleasantly friendly and casual.

'But I couldn't have come anyway. I'm going out too.'

Max picked up a handful of needle packets and trickled them through his fingers. She watched the further waste of an hour's work, not caring in the least. She would have plenty of time for needles after he had gone.

'Ah, yes,' he said. 'John Morris. I'd almost forgotten him. Did he have a pleasant weekend in Scarborough?'

Sophy opened her mouth to say yes and paused. Had she said Scarborough? There was another town she always muddled it with. 'Harrogate,' she uttered triumphantly. 'It was Harrogate.'

Max's lips twitched. 'So it was. I always muddle those two towns. I must visit them one day, then perhaps I shall be able to tell them apart. Perhaps you'll invite me when you're married,' he added slyly.

Sophy looked at him appalled, her gentle mouth slightly open. 'Married?' she echoed, stupidly.

He raised black brows. 'My dear girl! I hardly imagine that you intend to live in sin, do you?'

'Live in sin—who with?'

'How you do keep repeating my words. But don't look so shocked; I'm only teasing you. I'm sure John

Morris would never hear of it.' He grinned at her and got up and went to the door. 'I'll see you before I go. Goodbye, Sophy.'

She said goodbye in a faint voice and sat down to sort the needles once more. He had sounded glad to be going back—he would forget her the moment he got into that big Bentley and slid away out of her life. She sniffed, blew her nose and wiped away two tears which had escaped unbidden on to her cheeks. She was on her way home when a dreadful thought struck her. Had he said John Morris—surely she had called the wretch Austin? She remembered that the name had popped into her head because it was a nice easy one, but then so was Morris. She consoled herself with the thought that if she could forget the name so easily, it was unlikely that Max would remember which it was either.

He came up to the theatre the next afternoon to say goodbye, Cooper and Bill Evans were with her and he made no effort to see her alone, but stood talking to them all for a few minutes and then shook hands with each of them and went away. Sophy hadn't expected it to be like that—the possibility of anyone else being there had never entered her head. She said everything proper to the occasion in her soft voice, and watched him walk away and out through the corridor doors; they swung to after him with a final thud.

Sophy's intention to forget Max was seriously hampered by the frequency with which his name cropped up in conversation. It seemed to her that everyone she met had something to say about him, both in hospital and at home, where she had returned on the evening of his departure, with a resolutely bright face, to find her grandmother arranging a vast quantity of flowers. She looked up from the lilac and carnations and roses, her charming face wreathed in smiles. 'Sophy! These have just come from Max—aren't they gorgeous? and such a lovely card with them.' She picked it up and passed it to her grand-daughter. 'His writing is rather difficult—perhaps you can read it better than I?'

Sophy looked at the familiar scrawl. 'Shocking, isn't it?' she said cheerfully, while the soundless voice inside her cried, 'Max—Max!' She swallowed the lump in her throat, and read obediently, 'A small memento of a friendship so happily begun, and which I hope to resume when circumstances permit. I shall miss you and Penny and Benjamin.'

'Charming,' breathed Grandmother Greenslade. She stood back to admire her efforts. 'There's tea in the pot, dear. I expect Max said goodbye to you at the hospital?'

Sophy poured tea, but made no effort to drink it. 'Oh, yes. He came up for a minute or two, and shook hands all round.'

Something in her voice caused her grandmother to pause in her work; she was about to speak when the telephone rang. 'I'll answer it,' said Sophy breath-lessly, but her hope died a quick death—it was Uncle Giles, wanting to talk about the fire.

'And how about you, my dear?' he wanted to know. 'There won't be any work for you for some time, I imagine.'

Sophy said she didn't know, and almost added that she didn't care either. She enquired at undue length as to her godfather's health, and then said mendaciously that her grandmother was waiting to speak to him, and escaped to her own room. Presently she emerged to get the supper, to all appearances her usual sensible, level-headed self. The conversation at supper was almost entirely of Max, and she joined in with an unwonted animation which caused Sinclair to waylay her in the hall to ask her if she was starting a cold.

'You look feverish, Miss Sophy,' he remarked quite anxiously. 'Not at all your old self.'

Sophy, assuring him that she was in the best of health, silently agreed with him—she wasn't her old self; she doubted if she would ever be that again.

Her work in the theatre was coming to an end; another few days and she would be starting relief duties. Staff Cooper was already posted to Cas; the junior nurses had been absorbed into the wards. The theatre was full of workmen.

It was the fifth morning after Max had left, and Saturday. The children didn't go to school; Grandmother Greenslade always breakfasted in bed anyway; Sinclair was away for a day or two on one of his rare visits to a brother. Sophy had the early morning to herself in the quiet house. She picked up the post as she crossed the hall to the kitchen to make herself some tea. There were bills, of course, and a letter from Aunt Vera and, right at the bottom, a letter from Max. She put the rest of the letters down, and stood looking at it in her hand. It wasn't until she had made the tea that she opened it. It was headed Huys Oosterwelde, and then an outlandish name which she supposed was the village where he lived. She poured her tea and sat down, and forced herself to read the letter slowly. It was quite short.

Dear Sophy,
As you know, the theatre here was due to open upon my return. Unfortunately the Theatre Sister I am accustomed to work with has today gone into quarantine with measles. I have been offered several substitutes, but I do not care for unfamiliar faces around me. Would you consider taking over the job for a week or so, perhaps three weeks? I never could remember quarantine periods. You understand my foibles and know your job thoroughly. If you would agree to this I think it will be possible for me to arrange everything with the proper authorities.

Yours sincerely,
Max van Oosterwelde.

PS You need have no fears regarding language difficulties—those for whom you will work speak and understand basic English at least.

Sophy read this business-like letter through twice, then put it back into its envelope. She poured another cup of tea and drank it, and ate a slice of toast loaded with marmalade, then went through the rest of the letters with her usual efficient care. Then she read Max's letter once more, finding it extraordinary that she, who had been making decisions ever since her parents' death, was now quite unable to put two coherent thoughts together concerning the letter in her hand. She finished her tea, tidied up, and went upstairs to her grandmother's room with a cup of tea in one hand, and the letter in the other. Mrs Greenslade put down her inevitable crossword, accepted the tea and put up a pretty cheek to be kissed.

'I've had a letter from Max,' said Sophy without preamble, offering it to her grandmother to read. Mrs Greenslade read it to the end, and then, as most women do, turned it over to make sure there was nothing else written on the other side. There wasn't. She read it through again, then looked thoughtfully at her granddaughter, perched like a little girl on the end of the bed. She put the letter down carefully, and said dryly,

'I am glad to see that Max has such a high regard of your work as Theatre Sister, darling. Shall you go?'

Sophy wanted to go very much; she pleated the bedspread with hands that shook. 'No,' she said at length. 'I shan't go. I daresay that Max is just being civil—there must be any number of nurses...'

Her grandmother interrupted her briskly. 'I'm sure you're right, dear, but even if you don't like the idea, think how much it will please Uncle Giles—he must be wanting to repay Max for all that he has done. Why not indulge his whim? It will be a few weeks at the most, and besides, you will be able to see Holland.'

Sophy stopped spoiling the bedspread. 'I should like to see Holland,' she remarked; she should have said Max instead of Holland; she pushed the thought away from her, and got up, smoothing down her dress. 'You think I should go, Granny?'

Mrs Greenslade passed the letter back and picked up the crossword again. She said gently, 'Yes, dar-

ling, I do. Even though you don't particularly want
to.'

Sophy had made herself late. She tore into her uniform, pinned her cap on to her neat hair, and started
for the office. The Board of Governors were meeting
later on; perhaps afterwards she might know more
about the theatre and her own future. She got to the
door just in time to lift the receiver. It was Uncle
Giles.

'Sophy? Have you heard from Max? You have—
good. I hope you will decide to go, my dear; it would
please me very much. Difficulties? No I don't imagine
so…these things can be arranged, you know.' He
went on talking at some length; he sounded pleased
and cheerful. When he rang off, Sophy went over to
the window and stood looking out on to the quadran-
gle, empty save for a few scurrying figures, anxious
to get in again out of the cold autumn wind. The
telephone rang again, and she went back to the desk
and picked up the receiver. She wasn't prepared for
the faintly accented English of Max's voice. She
blushed fierily, but that didn't matter—there was no
one to see, but the sudden loss of her breath was a
more serious matter.

'Have you been running?' he wanted to know, and
sounded as though he was laughing.

'Yes…no…you surprised me.'

'Have you not had my letter?'

She had mastered her traitor voice at last. 'Yes, this
morning.'

'You'll come.' It sounded more like a command.

Sophy smiled and nodded, for all the world as

though he were beside her. 'Yes, if you can't get anyone else.'

He let that pass. 'Good. I'll see to everything. Could you be ready by the day after tomorrow...no, tomorrow evening?'

Sophy felt as though someone had given her a push from behind at the top of an icy slope. Pride made her say in a soft reluctant voice, 'Well...I expect so,' though she would have jumped on to the next plane.

He laughed, and she wondered why.

'Will that give you time to see your boy-friend?' He was laughing again.

She said wildly, 'Yes, at least'—she thought rapidly—'I'll have to write to him. He's away—he won't mind.'

'I can think of no possible reason why he should mind.' His voice sounded arrogant and mildly bored.

Sophy frowned at the wall. 'Of course he'll mind,' she snapped, 'he won't be able to see me, will he?'

'I imagine that he will come over and see you if he wishes—after all, it's about the same distance to Harrogate as it is to Utrecht.'

Sophy, to whom this was news, could think of nothing to say; he didn't seem to expect an answer anyway, but plunged briskly into instructions, as to what she should do in order to arrive in Utrecht safely. Luckily she had kept her passport up to date— a reminder of the holiday they had all spent together in France before her parents died. When he had finished, she asked,

'And Matron?'

'I'll ring her now—she will send for you later, I expect.'

He was right—he was always right. Matron did send for her, and rather to her surprise everything was easy. Nobody either in England or Holland raised any objection to her going. Her journey and its fare would be taken care of, said Matron, and when she arrived at Schiphol she would be met by Jonkheer van Oosterwelde himself. Matron suggested the minimum of clothes, and added a rider concerning the wearing of warm underclothes. Holland, she had been given to understand, could be a good deal colder than England. Sophy, who had no intention of adding to the few flimsy garments which she wore beneath her prim uniform, said Yes, Matron, and went home to pack. In this task she was assisted by the entire household, each with their own ideas of what she should take with her. Finally she decided on the green tweed suit, and her thick tweed topcoat and a variety of sweaters. She added her lambswool shirtwaister, and, after careful thought, the amber silk; it was unlikely that she would need it—but still...

Her ticket arrived the next morning by special messenger; she was to leave by an early evening plane. It was Bill who took them all to the airport in his elderly Rover. Even with the luggage in the boot, it was a tight squeeze, for the lot accompanied them, as did Titus; but he, of course, took up no room, sitting composedly on Sophy's lap. Sophy had not flown before, and that in a way was a good thing, for there was so much to take her attention that the goodbyes were easier than she had anticipated. Anyway, she told herself, as she watched the ground sliding away from the plane's wheels, she would be back in a couple of weeks.

Schiphol was a pleasant surprise, with its welcoming lights and its air of good-natured bustle, and everyone looking reassuringly like the English. There was comfort in being addressed in her own tongue, too, even the porter who took her two cases tossed a 'Follow me, miss,' over his shoulder with the air of one who was familiar with the language. She listened to the jabber of sound around her—no wonder it was called double Dutch; she wondered if she would be able to master even a few words before she went back home, and thought not. She passed through the cheerful, efficient machinery of the Customs and so out into the main entrance hall. The place was full of people being kissed and greeted and exclaimed over; she suddenly felt very lonely and uncertain.

'Welcome to Holland,' said Max from behind her. She turned round, her smile so lovely that her face looked positively beautiful.

His blue eyes twinkled down at hers. 'Did you think that I wouldn't be here?' he asked, half laughing.

'No—yes—If you'd had a busy day…' She was so glad to see him again; the calm cool manner she had planned quite forgotten.

'I said that I would meet you, Sophy,' he reminded her mildly. He was shepherding her through the groups of people, an arm under her elbow. They went through the doors on to the pavement outside; there was a silver-grey Rolls-Royce drawn up to the kerb. Max opened the door, and said, 'Get in, I'll see to your bags.' Presently he slid into the seat beside her; he was wearing a topcoat, and looked enormous. Sophy looked ahead of her although there was nothing to see. They slid away down the dark road, the car's headlights picking out an occasional cottage, their beam competing with the rays of a half-hearted moon.

'It's half an hour or so to Utrecht,' said Max. 'I'm taking you straight to the hospital; someone will give you supper and show you your room. Do you feel you could start in theatre tomorrow? I'm not starting until eleven, that gives you time to look around; you'll find it almost identical with your own theatre.'

'I'm ready to start when you like,' said Sophy, 'but what about the nurses? Do they understand English?'

'Oh, yes, a word or two—but why should you need to speak to them? Surely your eyebrows will be just as eloquent here as in London?' He slowed the car to go through Amstelveen, and then shot ahead again. Presently the road eased itself on to the motorway between Amsterdam and Utrecht; Sophy watched the speedometer needle sweep round to the hundred and twenty mark, where Max kept it steady.

'How Ben would love this,' Sophy exclaimed.

'Yes, I imagine so—how are they all?'

There was, Sophy discovered, quite a lot to talk about. In no time at all the outskirts of Utrecht came trickling to meet them, and then they were passing between rows of tall houses with brightly lighted windows, and so to the busy shopping streets, surprisingly full of people. Sophy, obedient to Max's directions, gazed at the Dom tower and the university and a great many picturesque buildings, only dimly visible, and most of all at the canals, their inky waters sluggishly reflecting the city's lights; when they turned at last into a narrow quiet street, the silent darkness seemed almost dreamlike. But it was real

enough to Max; he scarcely slackened speed over the
cobblestones before passing through an open gate-
way, its wrought iron gates brightly lighted, and so
across a broad courtyard, to stop with quiet exactitude
before the hospital doors.

Sophy didn't have much time to look around her—
the hospital looked old; it could have been any one
of its London counterparts. They went inside, and
here again she felt on familiar ground, for the porter
who came to meet them out of his little box-like room
was very like Pratt. He spoke to Max and then said,
'Good evening, Sister.' Sophy answered him, looking
astonished, and Max smiled and said,

'Hans was in England during the last war—he'll
help you in any way he can.' He turned to the porter
and went on in Dutch, 'Send a man for Sister's luggage, will you'—he gave him the car keys—'I'll col-
lect them as I come back. Is Mevrouw van der Wijde
here?'

'Yes, Professor, in the consultants' room.' Max
nodded, took Sophy by the arm and turned down the
inevitable long hospital corridor. They didn't go far.
He stopped at a handsome door, opened it, and ushered Sophy inside. The room was large and comfortably and rather heavily furnished with large leather
chairs and a number of small writing tables. There
was a large bookcase along the length of one wall,
and a stove, giving out a comfortable warmth. It was
well lighted, but the heavy curtains draping the long
narrow windows were undrawn. Standing by the nearest window was a girl; she turned round as Sophy
went in and smiled at her. The smile was very sweet,
and Sophy thought she had never seen such a pretty

face before, or such vivid blue eyes. The girl spoke in an English that was only slightly accented. 'Max, I thought you were never coming.' She started to walk across the room towards them, still smiling.

'That sounds like a flattering remark,' said Max, 'but as I'm sure you forgot the time I asked you to be here, I'll not even answer it. Come and meet Miss Sophia Greenslade.' He turned to Sophy. 'This is Mevrouw van der Wijde; she knows all about you and wanted to meet you as soon as you arrived.'

The two girls shook hands, and Sophy answered a friendly fusillade of questions about her journey until Max interrupted quietly.

'The Directrice is expecting you; shall we go and see her now?' he suggested, and stood patiently while goodbyes were said, then opened the door for Sophy, pausing long enough to say over his shoulder, 'Wait for me here Tineke—the car's outside. I shan't be long.'

Sophy heard this remark with mixed feelings; it was obvious that she had arrived at a most awkward hour, Mevrouw van der Wijde was dressed for an evening out which had most certainly been delayed so that Max could fetch her from Schiphol...it was also obvious that this girl was the reason for Max not being available.

They walked down the corridor and he knocked on another door and ushered her inside. This time the room was small, and so was the woman who stood up to meet them. Sophy had imagined that all Dutch-women would be big and tall and blonde—Mevrouw van der Wijde's dainty prettiness had been a sur-prise—the Directrice was even more so, for not only was she a little woman, but her hair was almost black, as were her eyes. She nodded briskly at Max, and said, 'Professor—so you have brought the English Sister.' She shook hands with them both, and Sophy murmured 'How do you do' and was startled when the Directrice replied that she was very well indeed, and went on to hope that Sophy was well too. Her English was heavily accented and at times difficult to follow, but Sophy felt that she was in no position to pass judgment. Max waited until the courtesies had been satisfactorily dealt with, then said, 'You will excuse me, Directrice?'

They shook hands again before he turned to offer a hand to Sophy, who took it with an air of surprise which forced him to murmur, 'We shake hands a great deal in Holland—I should have warned you.'

Before she could think of anything to say, he had gone.

Sophy thought that she was going to like the Directrice—she was kind and helpful with an air of quiet authority, and seemed to know exactly the things Sophy wanted to know about. After an interview which satisfied them both, Sophy was handed over to Home Sister, whose appearance at last satisfied her idea of a typical Dutchwoman, for she was a round plump little person with pale hair and blue eyes set in a face as round as her person. Zuster Vroom's English was sparse, but what she lacked in vocabulary she made up for with enthusiasm. She showed Sophy her room and then enquired 'Eating?' Sophy, who was famished, had been hoping that someone would mention food. She said 'Yes, please,' in a voice that sounded so urgent that they went at once to a large dining

room on the ground floor where a rosy-faced girl of
enormous stature served her cheerfully with thick pea
soup, a pale pink blancmange and delicious coffee.
Sophy ate it all uncritically and was ready for Home
Sister when she returned. They went back to the
Nurses' Home together and stopped at one of its
many doors. Zuster Vroom flung it open, revealing a
pleasant sitting room, full of women. Sophy, pushed
gently from behind, entered reluctantly, then saw that
all the faces turned towards her were smiling. Zuster
Vroom, bustling around her like a tug making a good
job of it, said loudly, 'Here is the English Sister, Miss
Sophia Greenslade,' then stood back as they surged
forward. Sophy was forcibly reminded of Max's remark as she shook a dozen hands or more and repeated her 'How do you do' over and over again.
They each spoke to her too, although she couldn't
make sense of any of it; it was several days before
she found out that they were telling her their names...

Zuster Vroom waited until the last handshake had
been given. 'Bed now, tomorrow you meet again.'
Amid a flurry of goodnights, she led Sophy back to
her room. 'Sleep well—seven o'clock you stand up.'
She beamed warmly and left Sophy to her unpacking.

Half an hour later, sitting up in bed, Sophy scrib-
bled a brief letter home and switched out the light.
She wasn't very sleepy, but tomorrow would be a
difficult day. It had all been rather exciting; and how
kindly the other Sisters had welcomed her; as though
they really wanted her to feel at home. Against her
better judgment, she allowed her thoughts to stray to
Max. He had welcomed her too—in the same way as
a hard-pressed plumber would have welcomed his

mate—she thought wryly; and how ridiculous of her to imagine for one moment that his feelings towards her would ever be more than that. She blew her nose defiantly; she was really being very stupid, for she had known for weeks that there was a girl…had he not almost said so after Mary's efforts to attract him? Nothing was altered, only now she had met the girl, hadn't she? And a quite beautiful girl too, she told herself honestly, with the kind of perfection Max would expect in a wife.

With an effort she tore her thoughts away; they held no comfort for her, and self-pity was a weakness she despised. She closed her eyes, and presently slept.

CHAPTER SIX

SOPHY WAS AWAKE long before seven the next morning. Utrecht had a great many churches; all of them chimed the hours; most of them played delightful little tunes too, led by the seven great bells of the Dom and its magnificent carillon. Sophy, lying in bed listening to them, realised that she had no need of her alarm clock, and got up and dressed and was wondering what to do, when there was a tap on her door and two young women came in. She had met them both the previous evening, and tried in vain to remember their names, and when this proved impossible, she stood smiling at them, hoping they would speak first. They must have read her thoughts, for the taller of the two smiled back, revealing white teeth in a pretty mouth.

'It is all strange, is it not? We take you to *Ontbijt* and then the theatre. I am Janie Gerritsma, Men's Surgical, and this is Annie Visser, Women's Surgical.' She waved a hand at her companion—a small dark girl with black eyes. Sophy was glad to see that their uniform was very similar to her own, which Matron had insisted that she wore while she was in Utrecht. Only their caps were different—bonnet-shaped and hanging loose over their hair at the back—very becoming, thought Sophy, who nevertheless considered her own frilled muslin cap made her plain face rather more interesting.

The dining room was full of nurses, all looking exactly alike. Sophy wondered how she was going to tell the first-year nurses from the second-year nurses, and the second-year nurses from the third-year nurses, and those in turn from the Ward Sisters. Her two companions sat her down between them at a table at the far end of the room, and she was greeted by a chorus of good mornings. She looked around her with relief. So this was the Sisters' table; somehow or other she must remember their faces—their names would have to come later. She breakfasted off coffee, and slices of bread which she spread with butter and then, with some doubt, thin slices of cheese. There was sausage on the table too, and a rather red jam, but no marmalade; she decided to keep to the cheese and while she was eating it, derived an odd sort of comfort from the thought that Max was probably eating cheese too.

The theatre block was a splendid edifice; Max had never commented on the theatre in London; he must have found it deplorably old-fashioned. Perhaps the fire had been a blessing in disguise, and the new theatre would be as modern and well equipped as this one. She was alarmed to find that she really didn't care what the new theatre was like, and made haste to turn her rather unhappy thoughts to what she was doing. Max had been right, the nurses all spoke basic English, and with the aid of the dictionary she had had the forethought to bring with her, the difficulty of language was far less than she had expected. It was half past ten by the time she was satisfied that she knew her way about; and leaving the staff nurse to make sure the theatre was ready for the first case, she went into the Sister's office. This, she considered, was the one thing she couldn't quite approve of; it was a small cupboard-like room, with a desk and chair, a stool in one corner, and a magnificent wall fitment, built with an eye to keeping everything in its place at all times. She looked carefully at all the forms, each in its own little niche, and found a washbasin hidden behind a panel; all the drawers had labels, none of which she could understand. She would have to deal with that problem later. The only mirror in the room, above a set of shelves, was small and several inches too high for her. She stood on tip-toe, but she still couldn't see more than the top of her cap, and she was reaching out for the stool, with the idea of standing on it, when Max said behind her,

'Sister Smid is a foot taller than you; I'll get someone to hang another one for you...'

Sophy turned round to face him her heart hammering, furious that she had to blush every time she saw him. She said, in a carefully level voice, 'Please don't bother, sir; it isn't worth it for the short time I shall be here.'

He took no notice of this remark, merely raising his eyebrows and looking down his nose in a way which made her feel that her remark had been unnecessary. 'Do you like the theatre?' he asked. He had come to sit on the edge of the desk, and seemed to fill the little room.

'Very much. I hope Uncle Giles will be able to see it, and get our theatre rebuilt along the same lines.'

He had picked up the off-duty rota and didn't look at her. 'He will undoubtedly come and see it; in any case you can look forward to taking over a brand new one in London; though I don't suppose that is of great importance if you intend marrying soon.'

Sophy opened her mouth to reply, and realised that she had no idea what to say. To her surprise, for she hadn't seen him look up, he observed, 'You look surprised. Had you forgotten your Mr—er—Austin?'

'No,' said Sophy. Hadn't he called the wretched mythical creature Morris last time he had been mentioned? She wasn't sure.

'Have I said something to upset you?' Max asked blandly.

'No—no,' she said rather wildly, and plunged into a muddled speech in praise of her new surroundings. Max listened patiently while she repeated herself several times, and then said in a serious voice which belied the twinkle in his eyes, 'I'm glad you like it so much; I hope that you will be happy working here.'

He stood up. 'Come and meet Dr Vos, the anaesthetist, and my houseman Jan Jansen.' He held open the door and she went through and they walked down the short passage to the little anteroom leading to the anaesthetic room. 'Have they found a box for you to stand on?' he enquired. Sophy said, 'Yes, thank you, sir,' and there was no time for more. Dr Vos was surprisingly young, with vague blue eyes behind heavy horn-rimmed spectacles and not much hair. He looked studious; so did the house surgeon, who addressed her in pedantic English, bristling with long words. She excused herself after a minute, and went to scrub, and gown up in the unfamiliar green; she was putting on her gloves when Max came in, ready to scrub. He glanced at her; she looked composedly at him. It was always easier when she was masked.

'Quite happy?' he asked.

Sophy adjusted her glove over the sleeve of her gown. 'Perfectly, thank you, sir. I have asked Staff Nurse…no, Zuster Viske to scrub too.'

He raised his eyebrows. 'Unnecessary, surely,' he murmured, then turned his back and turned on the taps. She escaped to the theatre and absorbed herself setting her trolleys to rights and checking carefully with each nurse, so that she knew what each was doing. It wasn't until the patient was on the table and she stood watching the men arranging the towels that she had a moment of unexpected, unreasonable panic, instantly checked by Max's laconic voice asking her if she was ready.

It was a straightforward list; thyroidectomy, cholescystectomy, a colostomy and the inevitable appendix. After the first few minutes she quite forgot she was in a foreign country. The nurses knew their work, and Max was surprisingly right—they seemed to understand her eyebrows as well as her own nurses at home. Leaving nothing to chance, Sophy had arranged to double check the swabs by means of fingers as well as voices; it worked very well, but she promised herself that before she went to bed, she would learn to count up to twenty.

Max decided to have the coffee break after the first case. Sophy had noticed a room marked 'Chirurgen' opposite her office; she supposed the men would have their coffee there. It seemed not; as they left the theatre, Max said over his shoulder, 'We'll have it in your office, if you don't mind the crush, Sister.'

She realised the question was of no consequence; they were already crowding in through the office door, and she wasn't near enough to reply anyway. One of the nurses came out of the kitchen with a tray and Sophy took it from her and edged her way in and put it down on the desk and squeezed her small person round to the chair. There was more room then, because the men sat on the low windowsill until Jansen pulled up the stool to sit by Sophy and engage her in conversation. She suspected that he was trying to improve his English. Max and Dr Vos gave her a brief glance but made no attempt to rescue her, and she was compelled to spend her coffee break listening to Jansen's views on Dutch politics, about which she knew nothing anyway. The rest of the day passed quickly enough, with an easy afternoon list which finished at four-thirty. Max had said almost nothing to her and passed her on his way from the theatre with a cheerful but disinterested goodnight. She went off duty herself a short while after and found Gerritsma and Visser waiting for her. It was getting dark, but that didn't prevent them taking her on a sight-seeing tour of Utrecht. They took her to the Esplanade Restaurant where they had coffee and carefully explained where she would find the best shops, and which churches were worth a visit, and where she could buy a meal cheaply on her days off.

She was tired when she got back, which was just as well, as she fell fast asleep before she had too much time to think about Max. Indeed, for the next few days there was not much time to think of him or her own affairs. She developed a habit of avoiding him whenever possible which was easy enough, as he evinced no desire to exchange more than the common courtesies with her, and Jan Jansen could be relied upon to monopolise her during their coffee breaks. She grew heartily sick of answering his questions, and after a time began to ask questions of her own, so that she acquired a small vocabulary of useful words which she practised on everyone, even Max. She had learnt to count and took a childish pleasure in doing so in theatre, and in greeting the surgeons and Dr Vos in their own language when they arrived each day. They replied gravely enough, although on one occasion when Max had come into the scrub room on his own, he had not only acknowledged her greeting, but followed it up with something in his own language which she was quite unable to understand. She had asked him what he had said, and he had laughed and told her that he didn't think she was quite ready for the translation yet. He had looked at her in such a way that she had found herself blushing hatefully, and had escaped to the theatre as soon as she could.

She was to have a day off on Saturday, and on Friday afternoon, with only a short list, she found herself free by four o'clock. The men had gone, and she went in search of Viske, who would take over until Sunday morning; and then herself went off duty. The swing doors closed soundlessly behind her, and she started down the stairs trying to decide how she would fill in her evening. A walk, she supposed, and then she could wash her hair. She was on the ground floor by now, passing the rather grand doors leading to the committee room and consultants' room. The first was shut; Max was standing in the doorway of the second. 'We were just coming to look for you,' he said. He sounded quite friendly, and she stopped in front of him and he moved aside so that she could see another man with him. Almost the same height and almost as big, but somewhat younger, with black hair, beginning to silver at the edges and very bright blue eyes which twinkled delightfully. He had an astonishingly beaky nose, and wore spectacles.

'May I introduce Professor van Essen?' He had looked enquiringly at him as he said it; Sophy wondered why. 'Coenraad, this is Miss Sophia Greenslade.'

Sophy found herself smiling as they shook hands. 'I think I should explain at once why I asked Max to find you,' he said. 'I have an English wife who wants very much to meet you. She was also a nurse, you see, and when she heard that you were here, she asked me to find you and take you back with me to meet her. Max tells me you are off duty: Maybe you already have plans, but if you have not, will you not spend the evening with us? You must forgive the short notice, but we should very much like you to come…'

Sophy hesitated. She hadn't looked at Max, still standing in the doorway; she wondered if he would be going too. 'If you are wondering about clothes,' she heard the professor say gently, 'my wife and I are on our own this evening; we shan't change.'

She smiled suddenly at him, and became instantly a very pretty girl. 'I should love to come.'

'Good, shall we say half an hour? I'll be at the front door.' He turned to Max. 'What about you, Max? Is it any good asking you to come along?'

Sophy watched the frown gather on Max's face. 'Impossible, I'm afraid.'

His companion glanced at him and said smoothly,

'Ah, yes, Friday; I had forgotten.' His eye met Sophy's and she was able to say, 'I won't keep you waiting, Professor.' She went without saying goodbye to Max, for he didn't even look at her as she turned to go.

She was almost ready when Gerritsma knocked and walked in.

'You go out?' she enquired, then sat on the bed and said, 'Tell me about it.'

Sophy, busy with her face, told. Gerritsma nodded when she had finished.

'This professor; he is a well-known pediatrician in Amsterdam—he is nice—he is also from'…she paused, seeking a word, then tried in Dutch, 'From *Adel*—you understand?' she asked hopefully.

'No,' said Sophy. She put down her lipstick and got her dictionary and they looked at it together.

'Noble,' said Gerritsma; she sounded faintly reverent, 'He is the Baron Blankenaar van Essen.'

Sophy went back to the important business in hand, disappointingly unimpressed, and wondered why Max had introduced him as Professor van Essen. She was roused from her thoughts by the Dutch girl.

'Professor van Oosterwelde is also Jonkheer,' she was saying.

Sophy gave her reflection a long look. 'How plain you are, my dear,' she murmured, and then, so that Gerritsma would hear her, 'Yes, I know.' She paused, half way into her coat. There was something she wanted to know. 'Where does he go on Friday evenings?' she asked. She buttoned her coat, and glanced across at her friend, who looked uncomfortable. She had to know. 'Tell me,' said Sophy, 'but do be quick, I mustn't keep that nice man waiting.'

'Professor van Oosterwelde goes to his home.' Gerritsma stopped.

'Go on,' said Sophy. It was like waiting for the dentist to pull a tooth.

'He spends the weekends there; although he comes into hospital at once if he is needed.' Janie got up and went to the door. 'I only tell what I hear, you understand—always he has Mevrouw van der Wijde with him, for the weekend, as his guest.' She had her hand on the door now. 'They spend much time together, and always the weekends.' She opened the door, not looking at Sophy. 'I do not like to tell you this, Greenslade, but you ask, *niet waar*? I see you later—I hope you have much pleasure this evening.'

Sophy stood where she was. 'Much pleasure' was the last thing she felt like at the moment. Perhaps it wasn't true—on the other hand, Janie wasn't a gossip, nor was she unkind or spiteful. Sophy shook her head as if to shake her unhappy thoughts away, and went downstairs.

Professor van Essen was lounging by the front door, smoking a pipe and talking to Hans, with whom he appeared to be on the best of terms. He saw her coming and waved his pipe at her.

'There you are, punctual to the minute!'

It was cold outside; Sophy shivered in her thick tweed coat. It was nice to see the dark green Rolls-Royce parked by the door. It was on the tip of her tongue to ask him if all the professors of surgery in Holland owned Rolls-Royces, but she decided that it might sound rude.

He settled her in comfortably beside him, remarking in a comfortable voice, 'Now we shall soon be home. I live in Amsterdam, but it's only half an hour's run: it's a good fast road, but rather dull, I'm afraid.' He carried on a gentle conversation while they were driving through Utrecht, putting her at her ease, so that very soon she was chattering away as though she had known him for years. He drove very fast, and skilfully, with a calm placidity which she found very soothing, but when they reached the outskirts of Amsterdam he slowed down through the brightly lighted streets, so that she could see something of the city, and presently turned into the Heerengracht and drew up before an imposing old house facing the canal. They went up the double steps to a massive front door which could have withstood a siege, but yielded immediately to the professor's Yale key, swinging back to reveal a large square hall. Sophy, gently encouraged by the professor, stepped inside; it was like stepping into a bygone age. The black and white titles on the floor and the dark panelled walls were a fitting background for the massive pillow cupboard against one wall and the heavy side tables, each with its old Delft vase loaded with flowers. There was an ornately carved staircase curving up on one side; the professor's wife was sitting on its bottom step, waiting for them. She sprang up as they entered: a girl of Sophy's age and height, but there, Sophy noted without rancour, the resemblance ended, for this girl was lovely, with enormous brown eyes and vivid red hair, piled high. She was wearing a sapphire blue dress, very simple. 'Cashmere,' thought Sophy, watching its wearer flit across the smooth tiles and fling herself into her husband's arms. He caught her neatly, kissed her quickly, and turned her round to face Sophy. It was then that Sophy saw the baby—a very small baby—tucked under his mother's arm; he had his father's bright blue eyes, and for good measure a great deal of dark hair and an embryonic beaky nose. It was quite obvious that he had inherited his father's placid disposition as well, for he made no demur when he was transferred from one parent to the other.

'My love,' said the professor, 'here is Miss Sophia Greenslade come to spend a few hours with us.' He turned to Sophy. 'My wife, Adelaide.'

The girls shook hands. 'You are a dear to come at such short notice,' said Adelaide warmly, 'and we're both so glad you could,'

Sophy said, 'It's so kind of you to ask me, especially as I'm a complete stranger...'

'Oh, no. We know an awful lot about you—Max told us.'

There was a tiny pause and Sophy's cheeks became faintly pink, then the Baron said easily, 'What do you think of our son?'

Sophy put out a finger to have it grasped by a miniature hand. 'He's gorgeous,' she said. 'What is his name?'

'Coenraad,' said his mother, and looked at her husband and smiled. 'At least he was christened that. We call him Champers.'

'A little joke we had before he was born,' explained his father.

'I'll take Miss—no, I can't tell you Miss anything; I shall call you Sophy, do you mind?—upstairs and we'll have a drink before Champers goes to bed.'

Sophy was swept upstairs to a large and beautiful
bedroom, and her hostess sat on the bed and watched
her tidy herself, talking in her soft voice meanwhile.

'I hope you're hungry,' she said, 'for Coenraad eats
like a giant, and so do I.' She looked down at her
slim person with some satisfaction. 'I can eat anything.'

'So can I,' said Sophy, 'and I'm nearly always hungry, Baroness.'

Adelaide jumped off the bed. 'Will you call me
Adelaide? I know we've only just met, but if you call
me Baroness I feel matronly.'

They giggled comfortably together and went downstairs to join the Professor, who was sitting before the
fire in the drawing room, with his son draped across
a vast expanse of waistcoat. He got up as they entered
the room. 'If someone will take Champers, I'll get the
drinks,' he said.

Sophy found herself in an enormous velvet-covered
chair, with Champers gazing at her with sleepy blue
eyes from the hollow of her arm; every now and again
he smiled windily. They had just finished their drinks
when his tiny face creased alarmingly and his minus-
cule mouth opened to let out a man-sized roar. This
performance, not unnaturally, drew forth cries of admiration from his companions, and he was borne
away by his mother amidst praise of his sagacity in
knowing when his feed was due.

It was later in the evening, after they had dined
deliciously at a table set with silver and crystal and
fine china in a rather formal dining room. The Professor had excused himself to read his letters in the
study and make a telephone call to the hospital where

he was in charge of the children's clinic, and the two girls were alone. Conversation had not flagged the whole evening, but Max had not once been mentioned. Adelaide settled herself more comfortably opposite Sophy, and asked comfortably,

'What is Max van Oosterwelde like to work for?'

'Very nice,' said Sophy. 'Very neat and easy in theatre, and never throws his weight about.'

Adelaide nodded her head. 'I thought he would be,' she said. 'We see quite a lot of him, you know, he and Coenraad have been friends for years.' She looked across at her guest. 'He told us how he had met you…'

Sophy blushed. 'Did he?' She wriggled in her chair. 'I didn't think…we met once or twice outside the hospital—we share a godfather, perhaps you know?'

Adelaide appeared to have no difficulty in understanding this muddled speech. 'He's a lot older than you, isn't he?'

Sophy's pleasant voice had a faint edge to it. 'Oh no. I'm almost twenty-six, you know; Max is only thirty-nine.' She looked challengingly at her hostess, who met her gaze with one of complete innocence, and a request for a detailed account of the fire.

'For,' she said, 'you know what men are; Max didn't tell us the half of it.'

Sophy complied, rather haltingly at first; but after a little while, her tale began to glow with the warmth of her feeling for Max. When she had finished she looked rather shyly at Adelaide, suddenly uncertain as to whether she had given herself away. Apparently not. Adelaide was looking interested, but that was all.

'I should think he would be a tower of strength,' she commented, 'like Coenraad. What a pity he couldn't come tonight—but of course, it's Friday...' She glanced at Sophy, who returned her look steadily.

'I know about that,' she said. 'It was explained to me.' She watched the wary look on Adelaide's face change to one of relief.

'Oh, good,' Adelaide smiled cheerfully. 'I didn't know if you had been told—we don't talk about it, you see. Tineke van der Wijde is a dear, isn't she?'

Sophy drew a sharp breath; the conversation was getting difficult. She said. 'Yes, she is, and so pretty too,' and made haste to change the conversation, helped providentially by the return of the Professor. Max wasn't mentioned again that evening; and on their way back in the car, sitting between her new friends, Sophy joined in a conversation on a variety of topics, none of which held any pitfalls.

It was only later, when they had wished her a cheerful *Tot ziens* at the hospital entrance, that Sophy found time to wonder why Adelaide had been so very relieved when she had said that she knew all about Max and his friendship with Tineke van der Wijde, but thinking about it made her unhappy. She jumped into bed and started to write a long letter home.

She spent the next morning looking at the shops and even bought one or two things in an experimental fashion, and then went to the Esplanade Restaurant for coffee. It was large and cheerful and full of people. She ordered a second cup and sat sipping it while she painstakingly pored over the headlines of a Dutch newspaper; it took a long while to puzzle out even one line with the aid of her dictionary, but it was surprising how fast she was acquiring new words.

She glanced up idly as she folded the paper, preparing to go. Tineke van der Wijde and Max were sitting together at a table against the farthest wall. Their heads were very close together, and they were deep in talk. Sophy put her coffee cup gently back into its saucer, aware of a pain that was almost physical at the sight of them both. She buttoned her coat and pulled on her gloves—she would feel better outside, where she wouldn't be able to see them. She got up; they were unlikely to see her, and she wouldn't have to pass their table. Max turned his head, and their eyes met for a brief moment before she turned away quickly and made for the entrance. Once there, she stepped outside briskly, unaware of where she was going. After a little while, she found herself in the Agnietenstraat. She stopped and looked about her; someone had told her that the Central Museum should be visited and it was right before her. She went inside, bought a guide book and concentrated fiercely upon its contents; forcing herself to take an interest in the lovely things on display. By the end of the afternoon she had learned quite a lot about old Dutch silver and porcelain, and still more about a great many paintings. It was a pity that all this extra information had in no way prevented her from thinking about Max to the exclusion of everything else.

CHAPTER SEVEN

SOPHY, TO HER surprise, slept soundly, although her
last waking thought had been of Max and Tineke van
der Wijde; and any further thinking was effectively
prevented by the sudden rush of work in the theatre.
Nothing serious—at least not serious enough to ne-
cessitate Max's presence—but the sudden spate of appendices requiring immediate attention, interlarded
with two boys who had fallen through a plate glass
window, kept everyone in the theatre busy for the
greater part of the day. She was free at five o'clock,
however, and wandered rather aimlessly across to her
room, to be immediately pounced upon when she got
there by Janie and Annie, who stood over her while
she changed her clothes, and walked her briskly
through the quiet, chilly streets to one of the ancient
earthworks on the perimeter of the city's encircling
canal. They stopped before an old and picturesque
building, and Janie opened its door with the air of a
benevolent conjuror, took Sophy by the arm and drew
her inside. They paused just inside the door, and Annie whispered, 'This is a pest house,' and Sophy gave
her a startled look, then smiled when Annie went on,
'Built in 1567.' She was a stickler for facts.

There weren't many people there, and they sat at
the back, with Sophy in the middle having the hymns
found for her as though she was a small girl who
hadn't learnt to read. The hymns were sung rather

136

slowly, several to tunes which she knew, which made it all seem very much like home. She felt faintly sad, but then forgot it in watching the gloved sidesmen gathering their collections into the little velvet bags hanging at the end of the long cane each of them carried.

The sermon seemed long, doubtless because she couldn't understand a word of it, but she sat quietly, thinking about home and then, presently, about Max. She would be seeing him in the morning—she smiled at the thought and caught the frowning eye of a severe-looking Matron who stared at her in a shocked way before transferring her own gaze to the preacher.

The next morning was grey and wet. Sophy, pinning on her cap, studied her face in the mirror; it looked as washed-out as the weather outside. She gave the cap a final tweak. It was fortunate that she would be wearing a mask for most of the day. She went down to the dining room; exchanged laborious greetings with her neighbours, and ate her bread and butter and cheese without any appetite. She was crossing the entrance hall, feeling morose, when Hans called to her.

'Sister Greenslade, there are many letters for you.' He produced a sizeable bundle and handed them to her with a beaming smile. 'It is your birthday?'

Sophy beamed back at him. 'Well, as a matter of fact, it is, Hans. What a lovely lot of letters; thank you.'

She quickened her steps. She wouldn't have time to open the letters before the list started; she would leave them in the little office and look at them at her leisure. She put them in a drawer and went along to the sluice and the sterilising room and the anaesthetic room to make sure that everything was in readiness. She could see Zuster Fiske through the window in the theatre door, putting the finishing touches to the instrument trolleys. She looked up and waved and Sophy waved back before collecting the other nurses for the day's briefing. It still surprised her that they could understand her as easily as she could them—basic English, helped out with a few essential words from the dictionary, was proving highly satisfactory.

She went along to scrub up and then into theatre to get the sutures ready and count out the swabs. It would be a long morning; the list was a heavy one. She checked the instruments and started to lay up the Mayo table as the patient was wheeled in. The anaesthetist was someone she hadn't met before—she looked at him warily over her mask and essayed a 'Dag, Docteur.'

He looked up, his eyes crinkling into a smile. He said very correctly, 'How do you do, Sister Greenslade. You see, I know all about you. I'm van Steen.'

The porters went away, and he twiddled some knobs on the Boyle's and started to insert an intratracheal tube with great care.

Sophy paused to watch him. 'How do you do, sir?' she replied formally, and then in her usual friendly voice, 'What a relief—I was afraid you would speak Dutch; though I can't think why I worried, for everyone I've met speaks English.'

He pulled up a stool and sat down, keeping a hand under his patient's jaw. 'We have to,' he said easily, 'our language is difficult...' He broke off as Max van Oosterwelde and Jan Jansen came in.

Max nodded at them and said carelessly, 'You've already introduced yourselves, I imagine.' He spoke to Dr van Steen and looked at Sophy, who busied herself with towels and towel clips and left the doctor to reply. The nurses had slipped quietly into their places; she looked with her usual calm around the theatre, making sure that everything was exactly as it should be, and carefully avoided Max's eye.

The first case dragged—what should have been a partial gastrectomy proved, of necessity, to be a total gastrectomy and a splenectomy to boot. Sophy, standing on her little platform, listened to the men talking quietly, trying to distinguish a word here and there without much success. From time to time, Max asked her for an instrument in English, but that was all. They went straight on to the second case, which went with textbook perfection, so that the nurses let out soundless sighs of relief as the patient was wheeled away. When Max peeled off his gloves and said, 'Coffee, I think, Sister,' they suddenly abandoned their silent watchfulness and sprung into an industrious activity, so that the theatre was already half cleared by the time the three men had strolled through the door.

Sophy, clearing away the used instruments, finished her task with deliberation even when the junior nurse came to tell her that she had carried in the coffee tray, and then went reluctantly down the broad corridor, pulling off her mask as she went. She flushed under the eyes of the men as she went in, hating herself for it, then felt better when Dr van Steen said cheerfully, 'We waited for you, Sister, although we are all thirsty.' He grinned at her. She saw that he had a nice face, almost ugly; brown and wrinkled like a monkey's. She liked him, and sat down, smiling at him and poured the coffee. It was Max, leaning over the desk and opening drawers to find some list or other, who found her letters. He looked at them without speaking—she had thrown them in in a hurry; they were scattered all over the drawer, unmistakably hers.

'Is it your birthday, Sophy?' He had left the drawer open, staring at her.

Sophy took a sip of coffee. 'Yes, as a matter of fact it is,' she said in a composed voice, and remembered that she had said exactly the same thing to Hans, only he had wished her a happy birthday in his jolly way, whereas Max, when he did speak, said merely, addressing the room at large, 'It seems that we must all wish Sister Greenslade Many Happy Returns of the day.' Which everyone did. Sophy thanked them quietly, finished her coffee, and on the pretext of something to do in theatre, left them. She had barely closed the door when Max turned to Jan.

'Get Hans on the telephone for me, will you?' and turned to Dr van Steen. 'I have an idea,' he said.

There was no more talk of birthdays that morning. The next case, a straightforward hernia, collapsed as Max was suturing. Sophy's quick eye had seen Dr van Steen switch on the oxygen, and she had a knife in her hand a split second before Max put out his hand for it and incised the patient's diaphragm. She nodded with approval—it was the best method, even if tiring for the surgeon. She laid up the Mayo table again with all the instruments he was likely to need, and arranged the gut neatly alongside them. Jan was clipping off bleeding points; Dr van Steen was giving artificial respiration. She wrung out some tetra cloths and covered the sutures, then signalled a nurse for more hot lotions; it would be a long business. Max was standing over the patient his hand out of sight, squeezing the heart with a gentle, regular rhythm. He said, without looking up, 'Sister, take the forceps as Jansen ties, please,' and Sophy went silently to unclip the Spencer-Wells as Jansen tied off. He did it quickly and well, and then rinsed his gloved hands and stood waiting to take over from Max while Sophy slipped back on to her box. After a minute, Max said,

'Right, Jan. Now,' and withdrew a careful hand as Jan relieved him.

Max turned away to rinse his hands in his turn, then straightened his back, towering over the little group round the table. 'How is it going?' he asked Dr van Steen, who, without pausing, said cheerfully,

'Got him in time, I think, don't you?' He looked down the table to Sophy and winked, his hand squeezing the rebreathing bag without stopping.

Max took over again, and Sophy threaded needles and rinsed some instruments. It was almost time to send some of the nurses to dinner; there were two more cases still to be done; luckily, the afternoon list was a short one, not due to start until two-thirty. Max said, as though she had voiced her thoughts aloud,

'We'll do the other cases after this and have some coffee and food sent up if you don't mind, Sister—what have I got this afternoon? Short stuff, if I remember aright.'

They finished the last case for the morning just as the nurses came back from second dinner. Sophy sent one of them to telephone for coffee and sandwiches

and then went herself to help the others in the welter
of clearing up. She supposed that she could get something to eat in the dining room, but that would have
to wait for another ten minutes or so. She was strip-
ping a trolley when Max came back, and said, as he
had said once before, 'Your coffee's getting cold, Sophy.'

She pushed her theatre cap to the back of her head
with the back of a hand filled with unused swabs. 'I'm
going down to the dining room,' she said, and added,
nicely mannered, 'Thank you, sir.'

He eyed her coolly. 'You'll kindly have coffee and
sandwiches with us, Sister Greenslade.'

Sophy put down the swabs. He was using a voice
she didn't care to disobey. With outward meekness
and secret annoyance she followed him to the office.
The desk was covered with coffee cups and a large
plate of sandwiches, and all these were overshadowed
by the largest bouquet of flowers Sophy had ever
seen.

'From us all,' said Max pleasantly. 'We haven't
exactly contributed to a happy day so far, have we?
We must see what can be done about it.' She pre-
sumed that he was talking about the afternoon list.
She thanked them rather shyly, bit hungrily into a
sandwich and observed,

'They're all straightforward cases this afternoon,
aren't they? I mean, there's no reason why we
shouldn't be finished on time, is there?'

'Are you going out this evening?' asked Jan.

Sophy looked surprised. 'Who? Me?' she asked,
forgetful of grammar. 'No.'

'Do you not celebrate birthdays in England?' Jan

wanted to know. 'In Holland they are important occasions. An outing or a party, and all the family forgather.'

Sophy said reasonably, 'But I can't have a party without people to come to it, can I, and it's not very nice weather for an outing. Besides, my family can't forgather, can they?'

'I thought that perhaps John—er—Austin, isn't it?—might have arranged to come over.' Max's voice was silky.

Sophy went pink; she had forgotten her mythical boy-friend. 'How could he?' she asked airily. 'Monday is such a busy day for bank managers.'

This interesting piece of information was received with polite murmurs from her companions. She avoided Max's eye, and drank her coffee.

'I should have thought,' said Jan, at his most deliberate, 'that Monday would be one of the slackest days for bank managers. You see, after the weekend…'

He got no further. Max interrupted him smoothly. 'Jan, I believe I've left my tobacco pouch in the car—slide down and get it, would you?'

He tossed his houseman the keys, caught Dr van Steen's eye and stared blandly back at him. Sophy had attacked the crockery on the tray and was on the way to the door with it. Dr van Steen, with his hand on the handle, said, 'You don't mind if we smoke, Sister?'

'Not a bit,' said Sophy cheerfully; she was thinking of her flowers. He closed the door behind her, and the men's eyes met.

'Stupid of me,' murmured Max. 'I remember now,

I left my pouch in the changing room.' They exchanged smiles as he got up.

It was a pity none of Sophy's new friends were off
duty that evening. She looked at her cards and arranged them carefully on her dressing table and then
went downstairs to the sitting room. She didn't know
any of the sisters there very well; she struggled with
a monosyllabic conversation for a little while, then
gave up apologetically and looked at the pictures in
Panorama. It was only six o'clock; the evening
stretched ahead, as dull as yesterday's cooked pota-
toes. She had just decided to wash her hair when
Home Sister poked her nice cosy face round the door.

'Zuster Greenslade, there are people—for you.' She
smiled kindly, and Sophy got up. Someone from the
theatre: she must have forgotten something.

Jan Jansen and Dr van Steen were standing in the
homely little hall.

'We have come to take you to a party—your party
for your birthday.' Dr van Steen laughed at her look
of complete surprise. 'How long will it take you to
dress?'

Sophy realised with something of a shock that they
were wearing dinner jackets.

'Where are we going?' she wanted to know.

'Surprise,' said Jan, 'you have to wait and see. You
have a pretty dress to wear?'

Sophy smiled happily. 'Yes, I have. I'll be twenty
minutes.'

She was as good as her word—or almost. It was
twenty-five minutes later when she joined them again,
the amber Thai silk covered with her serviceable
tweed coat. They whisked her into the cold evening

and into the Vauxhall Cavalier outside—Dr Van Steen's car, for he got behind the wheel and Sophy was squeezed next to him with Jan on the other side.

'When am I to know where I'm going?' begged Sophy.

'When we get there,' said Jan. 'I told you, it's a secret.'

She had no inkling of their direction, they were going along streets she didn't know, but presently they turned into the Amsterdamse Weg, until they left it for a narrow quiet road, running hand-in-hand with water. When they slowed down through Maarssen, she asked doubtfully.

'We're not going to Amsterdam, are we?'

Dr van Steen turned off the road on to an even narrower one which still followed the river haphazardly. 'We have arrived,' he said, and steered the car through big gates and up a short drive. There were lights ahead, Sophy could see the outlines of a large house, and as they drew up the front door was flung wide so that they stepped out into a pool of light. Sophy paused uncertainly to find herself hurried up the steps and into the glass vestibule whose inner door was being invitingly held open. She looked carefully at the man who was holding it—a manservant, she supposed and a stranger. She stepped past him into the magnificence of the hall with its oaken ceiling and linenfold panelling, and was suddenly certain who was the owner of its sombre richness. A pair of carved oaken doors were flung open on her left, and she turned to meet Max's quizzical gaze. He walked towards her, his elegance complementing the elegance of his surroundings, so that she became unhap-

pily aware of the tweed coat. There was the murmur
of a gently persuasive voice behind her and she thankfully shed the offending garment as Max said, 'That's
right, Goeden, hang it up somewhere for Miss Greenslade,' and then, 'How delightful you look, Sophy.'
He stood before her, a smile just curving his mouth.

Sophy strove for composure, and almost achieving
it said, 'Good evening, Doctor,' her beautiful eyebrows raised in faint enquiry.

'Oh dear,' he was faintly mocking, 'I forget my
manners—you must blame the effect of your charming gown. Good evening, Sister Greenslade.' Dr van
Steen and Jan had joined them, and Max nodded at
them.

'I was getting anxious, Karel, but of course that car
of yours only crawls...' The three men laughed, and
Sophy felt annoyed—they could at least tell her why
she was there. She asked, in a frigidly polite voice,
and they all looked at her, but it was Max who answered.

'Did we not tell you that a birthday in Holland is
a most important day? We decided to show you how
we celebrate it in our country.'

He caught her arm and drew her towards the double
doors through which he had come, with Goeden soft-
footed ahead to open them and allow Sophy a glimpse
of the room beyond, softly lit by a scattering of lamps
on the numerous tables—there was some sort of con-
cealed lighting in the cornice too, displaying the viv-
idness of the painted ceiling. There were about a
dozen people in the room. They turned and looked at
her as she stood in the doorway, and she caught her
breath in a loud gasp as they started to sing—it was

a short and rollicking verse and seemed to be directed at herself. She felt Max's hand, cool and firm, give her own a squeeze and as the singing stopped he murmured,

'That's for you, birthday girl—"Long shall she live in glory".' His eyes twinkled down into her surprised ones. 'And now everyone will shake you by the hand.'

He stood very close, introducing everyone in turn with a kind of casual good manners that made it easy for her.

It was delightful to see Adelaide again, too, and her smiling, placid husband, who, after a few minutes' gentle conversation with her, turned to Max, remarking that he wanted a few words with him later on. Sophy seized the opportunity to turn away and was instantly seized by Dr van Steen and Tineke; there was a short, dark man with them with an unpronounceable name who smiled at her with what she could only consider to be Don Juan charm, and begged her to call him Harry. He handed her a glass from a tray Gocden was carrying around, and Sophy sipped something which she didn't recognise but which tasted good, and began to laugh at Harry, who was amusing. She couldn't see Max any more, but Jan and a pretty fair-haired girl strolled over, and she began to enjoy herself, and even found the opportunity to look at the other women's dresses. She decided at a glance that none of them was off the peg. Adelaide, who had just rejoined them, was wearing a deceptively simple chiffon gown, its soft blue setting off her fiery hair to its best advantage, and Tineke, in black velvet, looked like a fairy-tale princess. Sophy sighed with relief that she had brought the amber silk with her after all—it wasn't couture, but she had no need to be ashamed of it. She smiled rather nicely at Harry, who took her glass and began, 'I say...' just as Goeden's mellow voice informed them that dinner was served. Harry put a hand on her arm and then took it away again as Max's voice behind her said pleasantly, 'My privilege, old fellow,' and tucked her hand under his arm. When she looked up at him he was smiling, although she thought she detected annoyance in his eyes.

The dining room was furnished with a restrained grandeur which she found intimidating, although she supposed, with her usual good sense, that if you dined in it every day of your life it wouldn't seem so at all. She sat on Max's right, with Jan on her other side, and afterwards she tried to remember what she ate and found that she had no idea—but she remembered that she was toasted in champagne.

The talk was general and pleasant, with a lot of laughter, and when presently Sophy fell silent, Max asked, under cover of the hubbub, 'What are you thinking, Sophy?'

She spooned an elaborate confection of ice cream and then sat looking at it. 'Mary,' she said. 'She would have loved this.' She made a small graceful gesture with one hand, embracing the guests and the stately room with its beautifully appointed table. 'She would...fit in, wouldn't she? She is so awfully pretty and she knows how to talk.' She was unconscious of the wistfulness of her own voice.

Max smiled. 'Pretty witty Mary,' and added, 'and quite wasted on me, I'm afraid.'

Sophy turned pink, and said ingenuously, 'Yes, that was a pity, wasn't it? But now I can quite understand why.' She glanced across the table to where Tineke was sitting, and Max's gaze, suddenly frowning, followed hers.

'So you understand...' he began. But Sophy was getting to her feet in obedience to the little nod from the tall old lady who had been sitting at the foot of the table.

The women broke into little groups in the drawing room, waiting for coffee and the men. Adelaide van Essen had drawn Sophy over to an inviting-looking sofa, but they had barely spoken two words together when Tineke joined them. 'Mevrouw Penninck wants to talk to you,' she told Sophy in her light, friendly voice. 'I'll take you over, if you like.'

Sophy found herself sitting beside the rather formidable old lady, being scrutinised through a pair of lorgnettes; but the eyes behind them were kind, so she remained still, waiting for the old lady to speak.

'Do you like the house, Miss Greenslade?'

The question was unexpected. Sophy hesitated and then said, 'I haven't seen a great deal of it, Mevrouw Penninck, but it appears to be very beautiful and, I imagine, old.' She remembered the linenfold panelling in the hall and commented on it, and her companion looked at her approvingly, and said in her stilted, almost faultless English,

'And what sort of a home do you come from, Miss Greenslade?'

Sophy hesitated once more, and Mevrouw Penninck said quickly, 'Am I being rude?—I have perhaps spoken incorrectly, my English is not often used.'

Sophy smiled one of her nice smiles. 'Not in the least rude,' she said. 'I wondered if you wanted to know about my people or the house I live in.'

'Both,' was the reply—'especially of the dog and the cat.' She saw the surprise on Sophy's face and said, 'My grandson—Max—you know, told me of them.'

It was nice to talk about her family and the house to someone who was so interested; she chattered on happily until Max came over to them.

'We're going to dance for a little while, Grandmother. Will you be quite happy sitting there? Sophy, come along—you must open the ball, you know.'

Someone had rolled up the beautiful circular carpet and pushed its faded magnificence under the big windows; somewhere or other a CD player had been started. Save for a careless enquiry as to whether she was enjoying herself, Max didn't speak, and at the end of the dance, handed her quite cheerfully to Jan. She saw him presently, dancing with Tineke; they were talking with the same intensity as she had seen in the restaurant. Perhaps it was that memory that made her dance several times with Harry. She had decided that she didn't like him very much after all, but he flattered her outrageously, and in some obscure way, she thought that it might be good for her ego. Even without him, she wouldn't have lacked for partners. Baron van Essen, quickstepping with an expertise she hadn't expected of him, remarked that her popularity was such that he was lucky to get her for a dance at all. It wasn't quite true, but she could have hugged him for saying it.

It was almost midnight when the party broke up and everyone made their way into the hall where coats and wraps were found and put on and farewells said. Sophy, once more in the tweed coat, found Harry beside her.

'I'll take you back,' he said cheerfully, and refused to listen when she explained that she would be going with Dr van Steen. She was getting faintly annoyed with his persistence when Max strolled over.

'Sophy, I'll take you back; Tineke wants to talk to Karel about some concert or other, and Jan can go with them. You won't mind waiting for a few minutes until everyone has gone, will you?' He looked at Harry. 'Nice of you to come at such short notice, Harry; a party's never the same without you.'

He made no attempt to move away, so that Sophy bade Harry goodbye with more friendliness than she would have done if she had been alone, and never hesitated when she was asked for her telephone number.

Harry joined the last of the guests, and Max waved them an airy goodbye from the great front door, told Goeden to fetch the car, and went back to where Sophy was standing, studying the family tree painted over the great fireplace on the centre wall. She was not, in fact, observing it very closely, but thinking of the journey back to hospital with Max. She felt sure that he would hardly notice her; which was as much as to say how she would like to be noticed. She remembered a little proverb about half a loaf being better than no bread: it seemed as though the half loaf was to be her portion. She said brightly as he joined her, 'This is interesting, isn't it?' and waved an arm at the crabbed writing.

He barely glanced at it. 'I should have thought you were too sensible a girl to have your head turned by someone as feather-brained as Harry.'

Sophy thought he was teasing, looked at his face and realised that he wasn't. He looked very angry indeed. She transferred her gaze back to the family tree as he continued bitingly,

'He's a good sort and great fun for a young giddy girl—but you…' He left the rest of the sentence, like a subtle insult, hanging in mid-air.

Sophy concentrated on the crabbed black letters on the wall before her. Maximillan van Oosterwelde, she read; born 1569; married Juliana van der Post. She read it several times, waiting for composure and the angry colour to leave her face. She drew a calming breath and said lightly, 'I found him amusing. You forgot, Doctor, that I am neither young nor giddy— even if I were, Plain Janes don't have their heads turned.'

'I am not aware that I called you a Plain Jane,' he said stiffly.

Sophy achieved a laugh. 'Nor did you,' she said cheerfully. 'But I am, you know. Anyway, Doctor, I can't see what business it is of yours.' She looked at him, opening her beautiful eyes, with their impossible eyelashes, very wide, so that he could see that she was angry too. He stared back at her; his eyes narrowed, so that she was unable to read their expression. He said coolly,

'I stand in some sort of *loco parentis* to you while you are in Holland.'

The colour she had so successfully banished came flooding back into her cheeks. 'Unasked and unnecessary,' she snapped. 'I'm able to look after myself.'

He laughed. 'And what does your Mr John Austin say to that, I wonder?' She gave him a sharp glance and met his mocking eyes. He said softly,

'John Austin alias Morris. You should have chosen a better name, Sophy, but I didn't give you much time, did I? And a bank manager from Harrogate— my dear girl you did let your imagination run away with you!'

Sophy fixed her eyes on the family tree once more; she was really getting to know it rather well. 'How did you find out?' she asked gruffly.

He shrugged wide shoulders. 'You're a poor liar. Now, about Harry...'

Sophy swallowed the lump in her throat; she felt silly and humiliated, to burst into tears would have been a great comfort. She held them back resolutely, and was rewarded by the sound of Goeden's measured tread crossing the hall, and said the first thing that came into her head, 'I wonder what Juliana van der Post was like?'

She heard Max laugh. 'Snub-nosed and a cast in one eye, if we are to believe the family picture gallery. Maximillan loved her to distraction.'

Sophy didn't answer, but said goodnight to Goeden and went out to the waiting car, where she began a polite conversation about a variety of subjects, barely pausing for Max's occasional Yes or No. But as they were approaching Utrecht he suddenly said, 'My good girl, must you chat so persistently? Do stop!'

She stopped. Then in rather a quavery voice. 'I was always taught that it was ill-mannered to ignore your companion.'

He ground the car to a halt on the side of the almost empty road. 'Then I must rectify my ill manners at once.' He pulled her quite urgently towards him and tilted her face up to meet his, and kissed her with a fierceness that took her breath. Then without a word, he drove on.

At the hospital she had the door open before he could reach across her and with one foot poised outside the car, said breathlessly,

'Thank you for a lovely party, sir. It was very kind of you to arrange it. Goodnight.'

She didn't wait, and heard him laughing as she fled inside, where Hans, who was on night duty, popped his cheerful face out of his little office and asked her if she had had a nice birthday. Sophy nodded, not trusting herself to speak, and fled through the hospital too, as though Max were after her. When she reached her room, she undressed in seconds, washed her face and dragged the pins from her hair and got into bed as though it was vital that she should not miss a single minute of her night's sleep. It was a pity that she stayed awake all night.

CHAPTER EIGHT

SHE LOOKED simply frightful in the morning. The dark patches under her eyes emphasised just how washed-out was her face—she applied make-up with a lavish hand and then rubbed most of it off again; it merely served to show up the haggishness of her appearance. But strangely, it didn't matter. At breakfast she was greeted with a frank friendly envy, a good deal of sympathy because she had to go on duty, and a great many questions. Apparently everyone knew about the party; now they wanted to know how many guests there had been, and who they were and what the women wore, and whether the house was as beautiful as rumour would have. Sophy answered as best she could, in her curious mixture of basic English, sign language and a repetitive use of the few Dutch words she had managed to learn.

It didn't matter in the theatre either; she was gowned and masked before the men arrived. Karel van Steen was the first to greet her as he accompanied the trolley with the first case into the theatre. He twiddled the knobs on his machine until the little coloured balls were exactly where he wanted them in their glass panels, and talked idly of the party, seemingly unnoticing of Sophy's short, quiet replies. When Max came in, with Jan talking earnestly at his heels, she stopped in mid-sentence, said her good mornings in a stiff voice, and then lapsed into silence, taking care

155

not to look at Max. Not that it would have mattered, for he made no attempt to look at her, but plunged into his work with businesslike concentration.

It was while the surgeons were being gowned for the second case that Dr van Steen bent over the patient on the table between them, said to Sophy,

'You're free tomorrow evening, aren't you?'

Sophy cast him a look of astonishment which he didn't see and said, 'Yes.'

'Tineke wanted to talk to you yesterday, but she didn't have much chance. She wondered if you would spend tomorrow evening with her. She thought a run up to Spakenburg and then a meal at Hilversum. Her car's not functioning, so I'll take you both in mine.'

Sophy hesitated, and he saw it and said gently, 'I believe we should all enjoy it.'

Sophy, aware of Max standing close by, pulling on his rubber gloves with careful deliberation while he watched her, said, with an enthusiasm she didn't quite feel, 'That sounds delightful. Thank you, I should like to come.'

Dr van Steen said 'Good,' and then, 'Ready when you are, Max.'

The first case had gone smoothly. The second one had a jinx on it, right from the start. Jan got himself unsterile and had to be regowned, so that Sophy had to lean rather precariously over her trolley and hold the Spencer-Wells forceps while Max tied off, and then one of the nurses, stepping backwards, knocked over a swab bucket with a subdued crash which sounded thunderous in the quiet theatre, scattering its contents, so that the nurse had to creep around collecting swabs with her Cheatles, then do a recount with Sophy. Max ignored it all pointedly, and continued to talk to Karel van Steen, but Sophy was as aware of his irritation as if he had given her a sharp set-down; she wished in a way that he had, so that she could have felt resentful towards him. But she felt nothing but a professional sympathy when the straightforward operation for appendicitis turned out to be a Meckel's diverticulum, something with exactly similar symptoms, but which took a good deal longer to operate upon.

When at last the case was wheeled away, Max pulled off his gloves and said quietly, 'Five minutes for coffee, Sister,' then turned on his heel and strode away, with van Steen and Jan close behind. Sophy nodded to the junior nurse to follow them with the coffee tray, whipped off her own gloves and gown and went to scrub up again. Zuster Viske had already laid up the trolley for the next case, but the theatre had to be cleared and she had her sutures to prepare and the Mayo table to lay up; there would be no coffee for her that morning. Max was as good as his word. At the end of five minutes, he was back scrubbing up with Jan, and a minute or two later Dr van Steen came in with the patient. He settled down on his stool and looked at Sophy over his mask, and asked, 'Had coffee, Sophy?' and she shook her head and went on threading needles. At her nod, the nurses went in turn, one by one, for their own coffee; as the last one slid quietly back to her place in the theatre, Max asked silkily,

'I presume there is a good reason for the nurses' perambulations, Sister?'

Sophy passed him a Key's hernia director in a brisk

manner, and said, no less briskly, 'Nurses are having their coffee, sir.'

He used the director, gave it back, and put his knife gently on the Mayo table before putting his hand out for gut. He said softly with an edge to his voice, 'A—demonstration against my lack of consideration, perhaps.' His eyes were bright, she met them with her own bewildered ones. 'You felt that I needed a reminder of it.'

Sophy held out the needle holder and he took it unhurriedly. She started to speak, but found to her horror that her throat was so full of sudden tears that she was unable to do so. She wiped the stitch scissors with tremendous care and put them within Jan's reach, heard with a wild relief Dr van Steen's cheerful voice embarking on some trivial argument which none the less needed a reply from Max, and gave her time to pull herself together. By the time the case had gone back to the ward, and the next and last one had been wheeled in, she was her usual calm, pleasant self. It was much later, when the afternoon list was finished and she was sitting in the cramped little office writing up the operation book, that Max came back into the theatre block and stopped at the open door. He stood looking at her, very much at his ease. She felt the colour creep into her face, but she held the pen steady in her hand and gave him a bright professional smile, and waited for him to speak.

'I apologise for this morning, Sophy—I was in a filthy temper, but I had no right to visit it on your innocent head.'

She smiled again; this time the warm friendly smile that had the power to change her face so much. She said quietly, 'That's all right, sir, the second case was troublesome.'

'The second case had nothing to do with it,' he said succinctly. 'I was in a filthy temper long before that…since last night, in fact.'

Sophy studied her neat handwriting in the book before her, and said carefully, 'That's quite all right too, sir.'

'Is it?' he asked, and something in his voice made her look up. He wasn't apologetic any more; he looked sure of himself and very much master of the situation, and he was smiling.

Her heart had jumped into her throat; she gulped it back, unable to look away from him. He settled himself more comfortably against the door frame and put his hands in his pockets.

'There is something I must tell you,' he began, 'about Tineke and…'

He broke off as the telephone rang and Sophy picked up the receiver, not sure if she was glad of the interruption or not, and said, 'Sister Greenslade, Theatre,' listened to the voice the other end, then said, 'Yes, Directrice,' and put the receiver back and got to her feet.

'The Directrice wants me in the office at once. I must go.' She looked at Max, hesitating, said 'Goodnight sir,' and went quickly past him without another word.

Max wasn't in theatre the following morning. Dr Vos was anaesthetising for a surgeon she hadn't met before. He was younger than Max and put her at her ease in excellent English and with a facile charm. She was pleasantly friendly with him, her mind full of Max. He had been going to tell her something the previous evening, and although she didn't want to think about it, she would have to, for she was sure that she knew what it was he had been going to say. The remembrance of his kiss was still vivid in her thoughts, and just as vivid was the memory of her own instinctive, unguarded response to it. He liked her enough to tell her about Tineke, and he would do it with great tact and kindliness, unaware that their friendship was anything but a casual one, brought about by circumstances. He had to be civil to her anyway, because of Uncle Giles…and the fire; emergencies like that made people more friendly than they might have been. She suddenly knew that she couldn't bear to hear Max tell her about Tineke; she would take care to keep out of his way.

They met that evening in the entrance hall under Hans' fatherly eye. She was on her way to spend her promised evening with Tineke and Karel van Steen, dressed in the lambswool shirtwaister. It was a tawny colour, and went very well with the tweed coat, and she had fastened a velvet bow in her hair to give its mousiness a glow. Max caught her hand as they met and brought her to a halt and stood looking down at her, smiling.

'Sophy, I want to talk to you.'

She steadied her breath, silently deploring her dreadful habit of blushing, and managed a bright smile. 'Good evening, sir… I…I can't stop now; I'm going out with Tineke.' She could have bitten out her tongue for reminding him.

'Yes, I know.' He was still holding her hand; not

smiling now, a crease between his black brows. She took her hand gently away, and glanced at Hans, staring curiously at them; she didn't think that he could hear, though.

'I'd much rather you didn't tell me,' she said steadily. 'Anyway, I know.'

The crease became a frown. 'You know? Who told you?'

She said quietly, 'That doesn't matter, does it?'

'No, but I didn't realise that it was—public knowledge.'

'I don't believe that that is so,' she replied seriously, 'and I'll not say anything…'

A car hooted outside, and she looked through the door and saw Dr van Steen waiting.

'I must go.'

'Yes, of course, don't let me keep you.' He was all at once polite and withdrawn. Hans opened the door, and she went outside without looking back. It was only after she had been squeezed between Tineke and Karel and they were sliding through Utrecht that she began to wonder why Max hadn't come out to the car with her; he had known that Tineke was there. She frowned, and Tineke asked 'Tired?' in her kind friendly voice. Sophy found it quite impossible not to like her, which, when she thought about it, was absurd.

They went straight to Spakenburg. For early November, the evening was light, with a bright wide sky, the lemon-coloured horizon casting a pale golden glow over the fields. Sophy found Spakenburg everything it should be. They left the car and walked around the harbour, and then, more briskly, for it was chilly, along the path beside the water towards the Ijsselmeer so that Sophy could get a good view of the fishermen's cottages on the other side of the harbour. There weren't many people about, but those that were wore their old-world costume with an unselfconscious pride, as though they didn't really belong in the twentieth century at all, and were faintly sorry for those that did. They looked content too. Sophy wondered what they thought of the tourists who came to stare, and said so out loud. Tineke stared at her, then said,

'Sophy, I believe you like Holland. I don't mean in the same way as the tourists do—they see the flowers and the costumes and the old houses, but you see the people, don't you, and I think you want to understand us too. How nice.'

She beamed at Sophy who said slowly, 'Yes, I do like Holland, though I know nothing of it.' And she thought of Max—Holland was his country and he loved it; so she wanted to love it too.

They walked her round, standing patiently while she gazed her fill at anything that took her fancy, and answering her questions until it was too dark to see anything very clearly, when Karel decided that they should go on to Hilversum, where he had booked a table for dinner at the Clarion. He took them along a quiet road alongside the dyke which led them eventually to Baarn and so to Hilversum, which even in the dark, looked delightful. The restaurant was delightful too. They dined deliciously and, Sophy thought, expensively, and with a leisure she seldom enjoyed in hospital.

It was ten o'clock when they got up to go and the cold smote them as they walked to the car. It was a crisp night, with a hint of frost to come, and a moon struggling to peer through large woolly clouds. It was only ten miles or so to Utrecht and they went fast, talking happily together. Tineke and Karel got on well together; they must have known each other for a long time. Karel had mentioned that he and Max had been firm friends since the time they were small boys, presumably he knew about Tineke and Max too.

Karel stopped the car outside the hospital entrance, and Sophy said her thanks and her goodnights and went inside to the dim entrance hall. There was no porter, and she wondered why, then saw the light streaming from the open doors of Casualty. He would be there, of course, helping with stretchers and being generally useful. She was almost level with the doors when Max came out. He stood still, looking huge against the gloom of the corridor, and saw her at the same time as she saw him. Her heart gave a joyful little leap when she noticed the look on his face; he looked glad—no, more than glad—to see her.

'Just the woman I want,' he said. He spoke as calmly as was his wont, but she sensed an urgency about his voice.

'There's an accident in—from a farm some miles out, so there's been a delay getting them here. The two men are beyond hope, I'm afraid, but I can save the girl, I think. The thing is, Night Super and Night Sister are both tied up in Cas—they're short of staff tonight; and I want to operate as soon as possible.'

So that was why he had looked so glad to see her. Sophy said in as calm a voice as his, 'Give me ten minutes to change, sir. What is it?'

'Amputation below knee—a girl, eighteen years

old.' He saw her wince. 'Yes, I know; but the bones are pulped for two inches at least. I'm afraid of gangrene—it happened in a farmyard, there's bound to be infection. She's had penicillin, of course, but I don't dare risk it. If I can operate now, I can at least save the knee. She's pretty fit and healthy. Jan's run in a litre of blood.' He turned away. 'See you in ten minutes, then?'

Nine minutes later Sophy was scrubbing up while a student nurse, Cheatle forceps in each hand, draped the trolleys for her and then fetched the instruments from the autoclave. Sophy was still arranging them in their neat, proscribed pattern when Dr Vos came in with the patient, and a minute later, Max and Jan Jansen. It didn't take long, and while they were waiting for the porters to come and wheel the girl away to Intensive Care, Sophy went round the table and looked at the unconscious young face. Such a pretty face too; it must have received a great many admiring glances; now the glances would be pitying.

Sophy nodded to the nurse to go with the patient and started clearing up. The men had gone, back to Cas, perhaps. She was quite alone, speeding around the theatre, making short work of it. She bundled the last of the sheets and towels into the laundry bin and went to the sink to scrub the instruments. Nurse would be back presently and could take over while she did the sharps and needles. She didn't hear Max until he was standing beside her and it was too late to do anything about the tell-tale stains on her cheeks. As she looked up, startled, two tears trickled down to blot themselves out in the folds of the mask she had pushed beneath her chin. She said simply, in a watery voice, 'She was only eighteen and so very pretty.' She picked up a corner of her gown and scrubbed the tears away. 'I'm sorry, but I didn't expect anyone back...'

Max said very gently, 'Sophy.'

The one word said a whole sentence of understanding. She thought confusedly that one day he would use that voice when one of his children came to him, hurt or frightened. She could have cried again at the thought. Max picked up a brush and began to scrub the instruments in the sink and after a minute she said in a little ghost of her usual voice,

'You can't do that, sir, it's—it's not proper.'

He didn't laugh. 'No, perhaps it's not, but neither is it proper that you should be here long after your bedtime.'

After that they worked together in friendly silence until the last instrument was done just as the nurse came back to sort them into their respective sets again. Sophy moved over to the sharps and needles waiting for her on the operating table, and Max followed her and helped her with those too. Presently they said goodnight to the nurse and Sophy took off her gown and went along to the office to get her cap and cuffs.

'What about some tea?' Max asked from the door, but when she turned to go back to the tiny kitchen, he said quickly, 'No, I'll get it while you write up your books.' He was back very quickly. 'You look surprised, do you not think that I can make tea?' Sophy shook her head, and smiled a little, and he added, 'You don't know me very well, Sophy.'

They drank their tea slowly, talking very little, but over their second cups, when Sophy began to look more cheerful, he said, 'That girl—our patient of this evening—shall have the finest leg I can get her. There's a chap I know in Vienna—I'll send her to him—in six months' time you won't be able to tell which leg is which.'

'I shan't be here to see her,' said Sophy flatly, 'but I know you'll do all you can for her.' She piled the cups and saucers together. 'Thank you for the tea, sir,' she said politely, and got up to go. 'Goodnight.' She was half way down the corridor when she turned round and walked back again to where he was still sitting in the office. 'You're a kind and good man, Doctor,' she said breathlessly, and went again, angry with herself for giving way to an impulse.

Hours later, in bed, she remembered that she had left him to wash up the tea cups. The idea of it made her smile, and she turned over and went to sleep, still smiling. She awoke before it was light and remembered that Zuster Smid was due back in nine days' time, which, she told herself sensibly, was a very good thing.

CHAPTER NINE

HARRY TELEPHONED the next afternoon. He had the
temerity to ring the theatre block direct, and it was
unfortunate that Max should have picked up the receiver. They were having a snatched cup of tea after
a hard list that had cut their dinner hour to a mere
fifteen minutes and Sophy was tired, so were Karel
and Jan. Only Max was his usual calm, unhurried self.
He took the call and passed the receiver to Sophy with
a quiet 'For you, Sister.' She had been struggling with
the off-duty rota while she drank her tea, and took it
with a little tut of annoyance at being disturbed. She
had almost forgotten Harry; now she listened help-
lessly to his invitation to the Concertgebouw in Amsterdam. He had tickets for the following evening, he
said, and they had been difficult to get. It would be
churlish to refuse. She accepted and put the receiver
back in its cradle and encountered Max's stare. Their
conversation at Huys Oosterwelde was very clear in
her mind and she saw by his little mocking smile that
he had remembered it too, and she blushed hotly under his cool blue eyes. He said genially. 'I must tell
Harry to ring the Nurses' Home next time,' and she
frowned, her silky brows making a thunderous black
line above indignant eyes. How dared he suppose that
there would be a next time, anyway? Couldn't he see
that she had been unable to refuse? Apparently he
couldn't, for he went on smoothly,

167

'I'm glad you're seeing something of Holland, Sophy. Amsterdam night life?' he queried lightly.

Sophy got up; there were still two more cases and
it was almost four o'clock.

'No,' she said pleasantly, 'there's a concert at the
Concertgebouw.' She pronounced it atrociously, but
no one drew attention to it. She tried so hard to twist
her tongue around the awkward words; they had, by
tacit consent, got into the habit of unravelling her mu-
tilated Dutch and correcting it unobtrusively as opportunity occurred, so that she wouldn't feel discouraged.

'Very nice, too,' Max was non-committal. Karel
gave a grunt which could have meant anything; she
could see that Jan Jansen was about to embark upon
one of the informative lectures he was so fond of
delivering. She took a step towards the door and said
repressively, 'No, Jan, I haven't time,' in exactly the
voice she used when Benjamin was being troublesome, and he grinned sheepishly. Max had opened the
door for her, and as she passed him their glances
met—his eyes were warm and dancing with laughter,
he said softly, 'Haste thee, Nymph, and take with thee
Jest and youthful Jollity...' He added, 'A misquota-
tion, but apt.'

Sophy paused in the doorway and thought hard.
'"And I leave you where you are, for I know that
wheresoe'er I go, others will punctually come for ever
and ever." That's misquoted too, but just as apt!' She
could hear him chuckling as she sped down the corridor.

They said little more to each other for the rest of
the afternoon. Max, leaving the skin sutures for Jan

to do on the last case, pulled off his, gloves, thanked Sophy quietly, said a careless '*Dag*' to the others, and went away. She went off duty herself an hour later, to be met by Janie and Annie who hustled her cheerfully to her room to change out of uniform, then took her to the cinema. It was a French film with Dutch sub-titles; a combination which kept her thoughts fully occupied for the next hour or so.

There was a letter from home the next morning. The list wasn't starting until nine o'clock—she would have time to skim through it before she scrubbed up. They were all well, wrote Grandmother Greenslade, although Sinclair had had a bad cold—the Blot and Titus were thriving. Penny had been to the theatre with Bill; Benjamin had broken the neighbours' window. There had been a letter from Uncle Giles, who was getting so much better that he was talking of work again, though they hadn't made much progress with the theatre. The small snippets of news made home seem very near. She put the letter in her pocket to read at her leisure, and wished Dr van Jong a cheerful good morning; he would be operating all day. She went to scrub up, carefully not wondering what Max was doing, and concentrating so fiercely on her job that van Jong, who was a hard taskmaster despite his charm, conceded to Dr Vos that she certainly knew her job, although she was a foreigner.

As the day advanced Sophy's reluctance to spend the evening with Harry grew. She went off duty, walking slowly, and as slowly got out of her uniform, bathed and changed into the lambswool dress; she seemed to have worn it rather a lot lately, but there was only a week left now, and she wasn't likely to go out much more.

Harry was waiting when she went downstairs to the entrance. He was sitting in a Karmann Ghia coupé, its vivid mustard yellow making a splodge of colour in the dusk-filled courtyard. Sophy, replying to his loud and hearty greeting with sedate friendliness, got into the car, thinking that it was exactly the sort of vehicle Harry might be expected to own. She told him so, and he laughed as though she had been very witty. It was easy to be gay in such cheerful company—he had bonhomie enough for two—and before they were clear of Utrecht Sophy's good spirits had reasserted themselves. Harry drove well and fast, with a light-hearted tendency to avoid accidents by a hair's breadth at the very last minute. Sophy held her breath to begin with, then decided that it would serve no good purpose to admit to nervousness. All the same, it was a relief when he fetched up safely near the Concertgebouw, parked the car, and then walked her the short distance to a café in a small side street, where they dined very well indeed on chicken on a spit, preceded by melon and followed by a *coûpe Clo-Clo*, a confection of whipped cream and chestnuts and ice cream which Sophy chose because she found the name amusing. Harry was amusing too and a delightful companion, and even though she knew his compliments weren't in the least sincere, it was pleasant to receive them.

They talked so much that they were very nearly late arriving at the Concertgebouw. Sophy barely had time to look around her before the performance started. It was Brahms, and she sat absorbed in the

music, forgetful of where she was or who she was
with. At the interval, her head still full of music, she
got up obediently and accompanied Harry to the bar,
which was crowded. He wedged her against the wall,
and turned to go to the bar.

'Stay where you are,' he said. 'Will a Dubonnet
suit you? It seems to me you need something to bring
you back to earth again.'

She wondered if she was being a dull companion
and if he was regretting his invitation. Perhaps Max
had been right after all. She stood very still, feeling
a little lost and conscious that her dress didn't quite
meet the occasion. She let her eyes roam, studying
the women's clothes. This enthralling pastime was
unexpectedly cut short by the appearance of a spotless
white shirt front most effectively blocking her view
of her surroundings. She went on staring at it as Max
spoke.

'Won't you join us, Sophy?'

She tilted her head, breathing rather fast and looking pink, but her voice was cool enough. 'Thank you,
no. Harry told me to wait.'

He cocked a mocking brow. 'And you're doing exactly what you are told? You surprise me.' He
sounded amused. 'Join us just the same. Harry will
find you.'

He caught her inexorably by the arm and made his
way through the groups of people to a small table.
Adelaide was there with her husband, so was Tineke
and sitting beside her, Karel van Steen. The other
member of the party, a good-looking woman in her
thirties, Max introduced as Professor van Essen's sister. Sophy felt shy; the women were in evening

clothes—simple, well-cut and exactly right for the occasion. The men, in black ties, looked right too—why couldn't Max have left her where she was? But apparently her clothes didn't matter; the circle around the table welcomed her wholeheartedly. She sat down on the chair Max provided for her, between Adelaide and Tineke.

'We saw you come in,' said Adelaide softly. 'We thought you were going to be late.'

Sophy knit puzzled brows. 'How did you know I was coming?' she enquired.

Adelaide was hunting in her bag for something and didn't look up. 'Oh, Max told us when he telephoned and asked if we had a place to spare in the loge. I had to get Coenraad's sister at the last minute to make up the numbers.'

She stopped as Harry arrived with the drinks. He seemed delighted to see them all; he gave Sophy her drink and barely waited for her thanks before plunging into animated conversation with Tineke. Sophy sipped her drink and wished that she had on the right sort of dress, then looked up to find Max's eye on her and knew by his expression that he knew what she was thinking and was amused.

The second part of the programme was Berlioz and ended far too quickly. Sophy followed Harry outside on to the pavement and almost at once lost him. She stood still, being bumped into and apologised to by everyone else, who had been sensible enough to hold hands or something. She teetered on to her toes, trying to see over people's heads without success, not sure what to do, and when Max appeared beside her, she turned to him with relief. 'Lost?' he asked.

'No, not really, but we got parted at the entrance—
I think we were going to the left,' she added hopefully.

He took her arm without a word, and made his way
slowly to the edge of the crowd, where they found
Harry. He waved when he saw them, and said cheerfully, 'What a mass of people—couldn't see you any-
where, Sophy, so I got out of it. I knew you'd find a
way sooner or later.' He nodded to Max. 'Lucky you
bumped into each other, wasn't it?' he observed light-
heartedly, then turned rather pointedly to Sophy.
'How about a nice little supper after all that? There's
a jolly good night club where we can dance for a few
hours.'

Sophy hesitated, shocked to find that she didn't
want to go, but before she could reply Max interposed, 'How fortunate that I'm here; it seems you
didn't get my message—I left it at the front door on
my way out. Zuster Viske's off with a heavy cold, so
you'll have to be on call from midnight.'

Sophy, relieved and faintly puzzled, heard the un-
mistakable ring of authority in his voice—one that
was seldom heard and as seldom disobeyed. She said
contritely, 'I'm sorry, Harry. I shall have to go
straight back, I'm afraid. I've spoilt your evening.'

He shrugged his shoulders and laughed a little, and
said with a good grace, 'You hospital people are all
alike: gluttons for work. We'd better go before the
place falls apart without you.'

The journey back was more or less silent. Harry
was just as charming, but it was all too obvious that
for him, at least, it had been a wasted evening. At the
hospital, he bade Sophy an airily friendly farewell,

with vague references to next time, but she knew that
he wouldn't ask her out again—girls who had to rush
back to work in the middle of an evening had no place
in his easy-going world. She waved to him from the
top of the steps and went inside, to be greeted by
Hans, who was on late duty. She had almost passed
him with a cheerful goodnight, when she remembered
Max's message, and asked about it. Hans looked
blank. 'There's been no such message, Sister. There
must be some mistake. Why, Zuster Viske was here
not an hour ago, posting a letter, and she told me she
was on call.'

Sophy went on up to her room, turning the oddness
of it all over in her mind. As she reached the top of
the stairs in the nurses' home, she saw Zuster Viske's
dressing-gowned figure flitting along ahead of her.
She came silently back when she heard Sophy's subdued call, and added to the oddness by assuring Sophy that she was in the best of health and most def-
initely on call for theatre.

Sophy went on duty the next morning, determined
to ask Max to explain things. She had a half day, for
he, for some reason, had changed the lists and there
was to be no operating that afternoon; she would have
to try and see him that morning. It seemed impossible,
however, for beyond a guarded good morning, she
had said a bare dozen words to him by coffee time.
She sat, drinking absent-mindedly from her mug,
while the three men discussed the next case. She was
about to get up and go back to theatre when Max said
casually to Karel and Jan,

'I believe Sister Greenslade wishes to speak to me
privately—would you two mind?'

When they had gone, he got to his feet, towering over her. 'Well, Sophy, I am waiting to hear your reproaches.'

She put her coffee mug down, so clumsily that a little of it spilt over the pristine whiteness of the blotter. 'You did it on purpose,' she said quietly, aware that she was saying aloud now what she had known all along.

'Are you surprised? I told you Harry wasn't your type.'

'You spoilt my evening,' she said in a small, fierce voice.

'Did I? Did I, Sophy? Look at me, my girl. That's better.'

Sophy stared back into the cool blue eyes. 'No, not really,' she said honestly.

Max nodded. 'That's better. What a pity your choice of boy-friends is so unsuitable. John Austin didn't do you much good, either, did he?'

Her face flamed, her eyes, usually so gentle, glinted with rage. She fought to keep the shake out of her voice, and almost succeeded. 'I amuse you, don't I? You enjoy watching me make a fool of myself.' She swallowed carefully, to ease the ache in her throat. 'I think I hate you!' She got up and walked to the door and went out without looking at him.

She was rigidly correct towards him in the theatre for the rest of the morning and was vexed to find that he didn't appear to notice it, indeed, from his own manner, they might never have had their conversation in the office. As she was leaving the theatre to go down to dinner, he called to her from the anaesthetic room where he was talking to Karel.

'Sister Greenslade, you have a half day, I believe.'

She stood still, not quite facing him, and said, 'Yes, sir,' in a colourless voice.

'Would you come to the Consultants' room at two o'clock? I have a surprise for you.'

'Is that an order, sir?' she asked.

'No, certainly not.'

'In that case you must excuse me, sir.' She walked on, her starched apron crackling; her head, with its flighty muslin cap, held very high. She thought she heard him chuckle as she went through the doors.

She was in her room changing into her tweed suit when there was a knock on the door. She called 'Come in,' and then, in her carefully learned Dutch, '*Kom Binnen*,' and Aunt Vera came in. Sophy, half in and half out of her skirt, stood poised on one stockinged leg, quite speechless with surprise.

Her aunt tripped across the room. 'Hullo, Sophy dear. Max told me you didn't want to go to the Consultants' room and suggested I got someone to show me where your room was.'

Sophy abandoned her skirt and embraced her aunt warmly. 'I can't believe it,' she said. 'How lovely to see you.' She paused. 'Did Max know you were here?'

Aunt Vera nodded happily. 'Of course. He arranged it all—he wanted to surprise you; we hadn't intended coming just yet, but he told your uncle that he thought you might be glad to see someone from home.'

Sophy bent down to pick up her skirt and hide her face. She recalled only too clearly that she had told

Max that she hated him, and all the while he had been planning this!

Aunt Vera had made herself comfortable on the side of the bed. 'Max and your uncle are poking around the theatre,' she said. 'They'll be at the front door at half past two and we'll all go back to Huys Oosterwelde together. We only arrived an hour or so ago; just in time for luncheon—oh, and Max says will I ask you if you would care to come to Huys Oosterwelde for the rest of the day—such an unnecessary message—but still, he seemed to think that you might have some other arrangements made…and of course, if you didn't know we were coming, you well might.'

Sophy was putting up her hair, sticking the pins in with a quite unnecessary ferocity. 'No,' she said quietly, 'I haven't anything else planned, and I should love to come with you.' She turned a brightly smiling face towards her visitor and started bombarding her with questions about home.

Her uncle and Max were talking to Hans when she and her aunt reached the hall. Uncle Giles gave her a hug and then held her away from him, the better to see her face.

'You look marvellous,' she smiled up at him.

'Can't say the same for you,' he growled. 'You look like a doused candle—Max working you too hard?'

'No—oh, no. It's delightful working here—isn't the theatre absolutely super?'

Max was talking to her aunt; Sophy gave her uncle's arm a little tug and started to walk towards them. She would have to speak to Max sooner or later; it

would be better to do it in company. It proved easy,
after all, for he spoke first.

'Hullo, Sophy—I'm so glad you're able to come.'

'Yes, so are we all,' said Aunt Vera, 'especially
after Max had gone to all that trouble to change the
list so that you could have a half day.'

Sophy caught her breath and cast a contrite glance
in Max's direction, but he wasn't looking at her.

In the car, she sat listening to her aunt spilling news
lavishly, and not hearing any of it, but presently the
conversation became general, and she found that Max
was deliberately drawing her more and more into the
talk, so that when they reached the house and her aunt
evinced a strong desire to be shown round it immediately, she had lost her initial embarrassment and
became wholeheartedly absorbed in the treasures Max
showed them. She looked at walnut hooped-back
chairs, cabinets, gilded and ornamented with marque-
try, and listened carefully while Max and her aunt
argued gently as to the exact dates of ball and claw
feet and the slightly later lion's paw, and then wandered off while they were still disputing to look at a
side table with quite different feet. She drew Max's
attention to this in a perfectly normal fashion before
she remembered that they had quarrelled. She immediately went pink and fixed her gaze with rapt attention on the table while he explained about pad feet.
When he had finished, she plucked up courage to look
at him and say 'Thank you, how interesting.' He returned her look with an expressionless face and eyes
dancing with laughter.

It was after a leisurely tea, taken around the fire in

a small sitting room that she found wholly delightful, that Aunt Vera brought up the subject of the dance.

'Which evening is it to be, Max?' she wanted to know. 'For we are only here for a week, if you remember.'

'I've sent out invitations for today week,' Max replied. 'I've asked around sixty people, most of whom find a Saturday evening the best for going out.'

Sophy sat quietly, studying her hands in her lap. She would be on duty until five o'clock next Saturday, and then on call for the night. She wouldn't be able to go. Her hands tightened their clasp of each other, as she realised that he hadn't invited her anyway.

Aunt Vera was speaking again. 'What shall you wear, Sophy?'

Sophy achieved a creditable smile. 'I shall be on duty; and on call for the night.' Even if he went down on his knees, she thought, I won't go.

'Sophy hasn't been invited yet,' said Max easily. 'I thought a surprise would be rather nice.' He looked directly at her; she could see him smiling in the lamplight. 'May I have the pleasure of your company at a dance next Saturday, Sophy?' he asked formally, but with a charm that made nonsense of her ideas of refusal.

All the same, she said with resolution, 'Thank you—but I shall be working,' and added pettishly, 'Did you not hear me telling Aunt Vera so?'

He countered her waspishness with urbanity. 'Well, you know, you come off duty at five o'clock—you will have three hours to dress; and I have already spoken to the Directrice about someone going on call in your place.'

Her aunt and uncle were watching with faint amusement, tempered with a trace of unease, but that didn't prevent her saying with some stubbornness, 'I haven't anything to wear.'

Max looked long-suffering, to infuriate her. 'That was a charming dress you wore the other evening...'

Aunt Vera pounced. 'What other evening?' she asked.

Sophy said quietly, 'Max had a party here—for my birthday.'

Her aunt sat up. 'Max, how kind of you!'

Sophy gave up. He had manoeuvred her into a trap, to get out of which she would either have to appear ungrateful, ill-mannered and ungracious, or give in. She gave in. She looked across to Max and said nicely, 'Thank you very much, I should like to come.'

He said briefly, 'Good,' and began a conversation with Uncle Giles about an entirely different subject, leaving her to recount the birthday party, down to the smallest detail, to Aunt Vera.

Tineke arrived half an hour later: Max introduced her, and she explained that she had intended to be there to meet them on their arrival but had been called away on an urgent errand. She had slipped a beautifully manicured hand under Max's arm as they stood talking to Uncle Giles and Sophy, seeing the look on her aunt's face, said softly under cover of the talk, 'Tineke is a very old friend of Max's. Isn't she pretty? She's a dear too,' she added generously.

Karel van Steen arrived shortly after, and she went upstairs with her aunt and prowled around the bedroom while Aunt Vera changed her dress, although Max had been at pains to say that no one was bothering to change. He hadn't seemed to notice Tineke's elegant appearance. Sophy was examining a very beautiful silver candlestick; she put it down gently and remarked, wholly without envy, 'What a beautiful home Max has.'

Her aunt agreed in an absent-minded fashion, then said, 'This Tineke—are she and Max going to be married?'

Sophy picked up a small coloured glass scent bottle and looked at it with unseeing eyes. 'I don't know; but I would imagine so. Tineke comes here a great deal and I'm told that they spend a lot of time together. No one has said anything—but I have that impression.'

Her aunt gave no answer to this, but asked, 'Have you no other dress, dear?'

'No, Aunt,' Sophy said tranquilly, pleased that she was hiding her feelings so successfully, 'but it doesn't matter in the least—there's no Prince Charming to fascinate.'

They went downstairs and joined the others for drinks and then went into the dining room, where she found that she was to sit between her uncle and Karel. She talked animatedly to them both, trying not to hear Tineke's pretty laugh followed by Max's deeper one.

After dinner they sat in the rather grand drawing room, talking, until someone suggested bridge, and Sophy looked at the lantern clock on the vast mantelpiece, wondering if she should go. When Max said blandly, 'You'd like to leave, I expect, Sophy,' she got hastily to her feet and made her adieux hurriedly

before going out into the hall, where Goeden stood
with her coat. Max had come with her, and they
walked to the door, saying nothing. Sophy pulled on
her gloves and shivered. She would have to apologise
on their way back for her rudeness that morning. It
seemed the opportunity she had been waiting for—
but it wasn't. Goeden, coming soft-footed behind
them, opened the door to disclose the car parked outside; he ran down the steps and opened the door and
waited expectedly, while Max stayed where he was,
by the door.

Sophy looked up at him, contemplating her gravely
from his height. She was unaware that she looked
both hurt and bewildered, but said with an absurd
childish politeness, 'Thank you for having me; it was
so nice to see my aunt and uncle again.'

'The pleasure was mine,' he answered in a voice
as grave as his face, 'though I regret that, in the light
of recent events, my invitation was so ill-timed.'

There was nothing to say to this; she wished him
goodnight in a small bleating voice, and got into the
car.

CHAPTER TEN

THE OPPORTUNITY to apologise came the very next day. The theatre had been going all the morning with what Sophy called knife-and-fork cases—too serious for Cas to tackle, but still simple enough for Jan to manage. She went down to a late dinner, and came back to find him in the office.

'There's an internal injuries in,' he said. 'He's having a transfusion now—ruptured kidney and probably some crushed gut as well—He fell off a roof.'

Sophy nodded. 'Shall you do it?' she asked in her usual composed way.

Jan looked startled. '*Hemel*, no! The Prof's coming in to have a look at him; he'll do it, of course. He'll be here any minute now; I'd better go down. I'll ring you as soon as I know something. You'll be ready?' He spoke anxiously.

'We'll be ready,' she assured him gravely. She watched him walking rather importantly through the swing doors, back into the hospital, then went unhurriedly to warn her nurses. She had two on as well as a theatre porter. She set about getting everything organised and didn't leave the theatre until it was quite ready.

There was no sign of the patient as she walked back to the office. Nobody had telephoned; she might as well sit down and learn a few more Dutch words while she was waiting. She opened the door and went inside. Max had already arrived. He was sitting at the desk with a case folder before him, scribbling in notes. He glanced up and said, 'No need to go, Sister,' as she turned to go out again, so she sat down quietly on the stool and looked her fill of his down-bent head, holding on to a thin veneer of composure—to have it instantly cracked.

'Why do you stare, Sophy?' he asked, without looking up.

'I—um—' She was going to say that she hadn't been staring, but it was stupid to lie about such a small thing. She remained silent while he put down his pen and sat back, his eyes searching her face. They were clear and very bright, but his face was tired and lined, but in her anxiety to get her apology over and done with, she ignored that and plunged into speech.

'I was rude to you the other day, sir. I beg your pardon for it—I had no right to speak to you as I did. I...'

He interrupted her carelessly. 'My dear good girl, you have a perfect right to say what you like, though it's blow hot, blow cold with you, isn't it?'

Sophy had no answer to that, for it was true. She had said that he was a good, kind man and within a few days had informed him that she hated him.

He spoke quietly into the silence. 'I dare say you have your reasons for your *volte-face*.' He picked up his pen again, and went on, 'I'll operate in fifteen minutes, Sister. Perhaps you'll be so good as to telephone my home.'

She did as she was bid silently and then handed him the receiver, saying, 'Goeden is on the line, sir.'

'Ask him to get Mevrouw van de Wijde, will you?' and then—'See that there's another litre of blood handy for this patient, please.'

She handed him the receiver again, 'Mevrouw van de Wijde, Doctor, and there's another litre already in the fridge.'

'Good; don't go, there's no need—I'm going to speak Dutch.'

She stood without a sound, listening to the gentleness of his voice as he talked with Tineke.

The case went surprisingly well—the patient was young and strong and Max, operating with his usual skilful patience, had the relaxed manner of a man who had all day before him with nothing to do; so that, when they had finished and Sophy made a rather stiff offer of tea, she was inordinately surprised when he said harshly,

'Tea, girl? When Tineke's downstairs waiting for me? I've no time to waste drinking tea!'

Sophy's ordinary face became animated by a gust of temper. 'Don't call me girl,' she said in a voice throbbing with rage.

He was already half-way to the door, but he stopped and looked at her over his shoulder, his mouth curved in a mocking smile, 'No? I don't recollect your encouraging me to call you anything else—should you prefer darling?'

It was difficult, the following morning, explaining away her wan looks to Uncle Giles, who had brought Aunt Vera into Utrecht to renew their acquaintance with that city.

He stared at his niece with a kindly, critical eye

and said forthrightly, 'Well, you never were a beauty, my dear—only when you smile—and you're quite out of looks this morning. I really must speak to Max; he's obviously overworking you.'

Sophy, who had no illusions about her looks, was not in the least put out by his remarks, but tucked a hand under his arm and said lightly, 'Nonsense, Uncle, he's a most considerate man. I didn't sleep; it's the unexpected excitement of seeing you again.'

This remark was accepted by Aunt Vera, and after some hesitation by her uncle, and no more was said as they made their way to the Van Baeren Museum, where they admired the patrician house and then the silver, but when they came to the paintings, Sophy wandered off on her own. She didn't care for dead game arranged artistically around apples and oranges and bottles of wine. She prowled around for a while until she found something to her taste; a group of small portraits by Lely, which she paused to admire, looking with pleasure at the smiling, placid faces, so content with their pearls and lace and satin gowns. Could they have been unhappy too? she wondered; perhaps they had learned to conceal their true feelings better than she.

'Nice, aren't they?' said Max, beside her. He glanced around. They were alone except for an attendant standing in the arched doorway, and looking the other way.

'I believe it's my turn to apologise,' he said blandly. 'I was in a filthy temper yesterday and I vented it upon you. I'm sorry, Sophy.' He waited for her to answer, and when she didn't he leaned forward and studied the portrait before them. 'Delightful, isn't she? I like her hair—pure mouse, wouldn't you say?'

She had got her breath back; she was able to answer. She said, 'Yes,' baldly, without looking at him.

'Am I forgiven?'

It was impossible to resist him. She said, 'Yes,' again, and moved a few steps away to look at the next painting, and heard him say on a laugh,

'My dear... Sophy, don't run away; for I have a second apology to make.'

She took her eyes from the painted ones before her, and met his squarely, and waited, pink-cheeked but self-possessed.

'It was unpardonable of me to spoil your evening with Harry. I'm sorry about that, although I should do exactly the same thing again if I saw fit.'

Sophy's eyes, with their incredible fringe of lashes, widened with amazement. 'If you saw fit?...' She stopped, aware that her voice was shrill.

Max surveyed her for a long moment and said at length, 'We never have time to talk, do we? But that won't last much longer.'

She thought he was referring to her leaving, and said without expression, 'I go in a week.'

He laughed again. 'That isn't what I meant, but it does remind me—Zuster Smid wants another week if she can be spared. Would you stay? Please, Sophy.'

She had meant to say no, but she said 'All right' in a meek voice she couldn't believe was hers, and he crushed her hand in one of his, so that she smiled with happiness at his touch, momentarily outshining the beauties on the wall, only to be at once extinguished by his next words.

'I must go—Tineke's waiting outside in the car.'
He smiled, so that her heart beat a tattoo against her
ribs even while she was swallowing disappointment.

'Yes, of course,' she said in a dry little voice.
'Goodbye.' She didn't watch him go, but stood staring at the wall, and presently went in search of her
uncle and aunt.

The week passed in a rush of work and brief outings
with her aunt and uncle. Each day she saw Max at
the hospital, where he treated her with a correct
friendliness that held a tinge of mockery; whether for
her or for himself, she was unable to determine. She
had supposed him to be tired, now she guessed that
he was worried, and wondered if it was the same
worry that was causing Dr van Steen's face to look
so strained and taut. She had dared to ask him one
afternoon when they were alone in the anaesthetic
room, and had been taken aback when, after staring
at her intently, he had said slowly,

'I have waited ten years for happiness, and now it
is almost certainly within my grasp, these last few
days of those years seem—difficult.' His nice wrinkled face broke into a smile. 'That is all.'

She had been fidgeting with the key on one of the
cylinders, and began to turn it absent-mindedly, and
he leaned over and took it from her and closed the
cylinder carefully.

'I didn't mean to pry,' she had said at length.

'No, I know that, Sophy. Though many less scru-
pulous women than you would have made it their
business to do so. You must have heard talk—yes?'

She had said 'Yes,' not quite understanding him

and unable to pursue the subject although she longed to know more.

By tea on Saturday she knew that she was going to be late for the dance. An hour earlier she had sent Zuster Viske off duty with a sore throat, a temperature of a hundred and three and a headache which hadn't prevented her from tearfully apologising for jeopardising Sophy's evening out. Sophy shook down the thermometer and said hearteningly, 'Pooh! It isn't the only dance I'll go to, you know. Anyway, I can go later when the night staff come on at eight.' She smiled cheerfully. She had no intention of letting Zuster Viske, dear kind girl that she was, worry unnecessarily.

It was well after eight when she left the theatre. There had been two cases since five o'clock—a perforated appendix and a strangulated hernia, and Dr van Jong had wanted coffee afterwards and kept her talking. She hadn't liked to explain in the face of his obvious attempts to make her feel at home.

Goeden, waiting patiently in the front hall, was discreetly sympathetic and assured her that he was prepared to wait for as long as she chose to take. Nevertheless, it was barely forty minutes later when she came downstairs again. She had bathed and dressed and wound her hair into its neat topknot, and taken a final look in the mirror. She would have liked to have spent more time on her face, but she had no doubt that she would pass muster in a crowd. She didn't expect to be the belle of the ball—she giggled at the idea, picked up her evening bag and her tweed coat, and sped down to the car.

It seemed as though every window was ablaze with

light when she got out of the car at Huys Oosterwelde; there was music too, but Goeden didn't give
her time to stand—he ushered her firmly inside and
handed her over to a smiling maid, who led her upstairs to a bedroom she hadn't seen before and took
her coat, putting it carefully on the chaise-longue with
a galaxy of furs. Sophy put on some more lipstick;
touched up her nondescript little nose with powder
and was led back downstairs, where Geoden had reap-
peared to open the great carved doors so that she
might go into the drawing room. It was pleasantly
full, with dancing couples circling the polished floor
and a small band, playing not too loudly, entrenched
on one side of the fireplace. Pleasant little retreats,
contrived from banked flowers and potted plants,
were scattered around the walls, and Sophy slipped
into the nearest of them. She couldn't see anyone she
knew, but over the heads of the dancers she caught a
glimpse of her aunt and uncle going through the doors
at the far end. Max was with them, and, she had no
doubt, Tineke. She was too shy to follow them so she
sat down composedly on the comfortable sofa, half
hidden from the dancers, to await their return. Ten
minutes later she saw Max's handsome grey head
above those of his guests as he made his way towards
her. When he reached her, he said quite sharply,

'Sophy, Goeden has only just found me. The hospital told me that you would be late when I telephoned earlier. How long have you been sitting here?'

Sophy thought that he looked annoyed, so she said
placatingly, 'Only about ten minutes. When I came
you were going through the doors at the end of the
room—I thought I'd wait until you came back.'

He dropped on to the couch beside her and she was relieved to see a faint smile turning up the corners of his mouth. 'Why in heaven's name didn't you come after me?'

She hesitated. 'Well, I...I didn't quite...'

He nodded as though she had completed the sentence. 'You're shy, aren't you?'

He smiled again, this time to take her breath away, leaving her unable to look away from him, unable, it seemed, to speak. He said softly, 'Your shyness, just like you yourself and all you say and do, is a never-ending delight to me.'

Sophy sat very still while the room spun—the chandelier became a glittering sun, the lamps a thousand stars. Through a jumble of thoughts which made no sense, she heard Max say, 'Come and have some supper; you must be famished,' in such an ordinary voice that for one terrible moment she thought that she had been dreaming, but although his voice was calm, his eyes were not. She got up obediently, saying, 'Yes. Thank you,' in a small voice, and presently found herself sitting at one of the tables in the dining room. Her aunt and uncle were there, with Tineke and Karel and Adelaide and Coenraad, and she was instantly engulfed in their cheerful light-hearted talk while Max went to get her some food. She ate her way through *Petites Bouchées Bohémienne*, *Terrine d'Anguille*, *Oeuf Nantua*, a Mirabelle ice and a selection of *petits fours*, which he had thoughtfully brought her, and drank the glass of champagne which he poured; living, for the moment at least, in a little bubble of happiness which held no problems.

She scooped up the last of her ice, and Max said,

'Shall I get you another one? I believe the strawberry ice is excellent.'

She said 'No, thank you,' remembering the sandwiches and strong tea they had shared on the night of the fire, and as though he had read her thoughts, he said,

'At least you didn't go to sleep in the middle.'

She laughed, and Uncle Giles said unexpectedly, 'That's better, Sophy, you haven't laughed like that since we came.' He got up. 'Now come and show me how to do these new-fangled dances.'

'No jiving,' said Max, 'and you've got one more dance after this one.'

'Which I shall have with my wife—the last waltz, if they still have anything as old-fashioned.'

'Indeed we shall have it, it's an excuse for the men to dance with their best girls.'

He glanced at Sophy and she felt the colour creeping over her face and said, to cover her confusion, 'Do let's go, Uncle Giles, I'm longing to dance.'

She didn't lack for partners. She was a good dancer and an even better listener; before long she was holding modest court between dances, quite unaware of her success. Max had not asked her to dance. She had seen him dancing with a variety of partners, and at least twice with Tineke. She was talking to Harry and a young man whose name she couldn't remember when Max said over her shoulder, 'There you are, Sophia, come along.' He had turned her around and danced her away before she could speak; when they had circled the room she said mildly,

'I was going to dance with Harry.' And then, before he could reply, 'Why did you call me Sophia?'

'You have always been Sophia to me—it is beautiful, as you are beautiful.'

She didn't dare to look at him. Of course it was absurd, no one had called her beautiful before, and she had the good sense to know that there was no reason for them to do so. All the same, it was delightful to hear Max say so.

'Our chance to talk,' said Max briefly, and led her through the glass door into the conservatory, which ran the length of the house. It smelled of spring, with its rows of daffodils and hyacinths and cyclamen and chrysanthemums, standing in Dutch orderliness. She would have lingered amongst them, but Max walked her down the length of it, and in through another door at the very end, to a small room with an old-fashioned stove against one wall, flanked by large comfortable chairs, and on the other wall a vast desk, partnered by a high-backed chair. There were a great many books on the shelves along the wall, and the desk was extremely neat. The only signs of luxury were the lush carpet underfoot and a corner cupboard housing a collection of silver. Sophy looked round with interest.

'Everything's very large,' she observed, 'but of course, this is your study, isn't it?'

Max didn't answer. Instead, he took her by the shoulders and turned her round to face him. 'Sophia,' he said, 'will you not drop your guard?' His cool blue-eyes, no longer cool, stared down into hers. 'Had you forgotten? I had not.'

She found her voice. 'No, I haven't forgotten,' and was swept close to be kissed, and kissed again. She said in a breathy little voice, 'Max—oh, Max!' and got no further. The door behind them had opened.

Max released her without haste and turned round. Tineke stood in the doorway, staring at them with a white face. She said in a high voice that cracked on a sob, 'I had to come. Max—' She started to speak rapidly in Dutch.

Max listened quietly, answered her briefly and then said in English to Sophy, barely looking at her, 'I'll explain later, Sophy.' His voice sounded angry and somehow urgent. He went without another word, sweeping Tineke with him.

Sophy sat down in one of the chairs by the stove, conscious of the sudden cold. Her mind was a blank, a fact she recognised with relief—it would be better not to think for a little while. Presently she got up; she would have to go back to the drawing room. She went through the door which Max, in his haste, had left ajar, and walked along the passage until it emerged, under a graceful archway, into the back of the hall. Max was standing by the front door, with Tineke, crying wildly, in his arms. Sophy turned on her heel, holding back tears and, worse, wild laughter. She walked back the way she had come, into the study and out of it into the conservatory until she came to the door of the drawing room. It looked exactly the same as it had five, ten minutes ago. She was surprised when Adelaide and Coenraad stopped dancing and came over to where she was standing. They stood directly in front of her, so that she was screened from the dancers, and Adelaide said quickly,

'Sophy, what's happened—are you ill?'

Sophy smiled from an ashen face; she felt peculiarly hollow but that was all. She said pleasantly, 'No, thank you—it's nothing that matters.'

Coenraad gave her a thoughtful glance through his glasses, his bright blue eyes very sharp. 'Let's dance,' he suggested.

Sophy began. 'No…' then stopped because her mouth was shaking.

'I think we should,' he persisted in his placid voice. 'We'll just amble round—you'll feel better presently.' He turned to his wife, 'You're dying to talk to Mevrouw Penninck, aren't you, my love?' They exchanged a look and he smiled faintly at her.

'Something happened to upset you?' he asked diffidently of Sophy.

'Yes—no.' Sophy checked a wild desire to burst into tears. 'I…I…it's such a muddle.'

'I see.' His voice was soothing. 'Do you want to talk about it?'

'No… You see, I don't think I understand, so I can't can I?'

He had danced her into the dining room, and she stood docilely drinking from the glass he had fetched her. After a minute or two, he said, 'That's better—would you like me to take you back to hospital? This'—he waved a hand towards the drawing room—'will go on until two or three o'clock, you know.'

Sophy studied her glass. 'Could I go before Max comes back?'

Coenraad evinced no surprise. 'Yes, of course. Tell everyone you're tired. We'll go and see your aunt and uncle and then I'll go and get the car.'

He was as good as his word. She had barely finished making her farewells when he was back beside her, making it surprisingly easy, saying exactly the right thing, joking a little. She wouldn't be seeing Uncle Giles and Aunt Vera again; at least, not until she returned to England herself, but, as she was careful to point out, that was only another week away.

They made their escape at last, and she sat thankfully silent in the car, while the professor kept up a flow of inconsequential talk that needed no reply. He got out too when they reached the hospital, and waited in the hall until she turned the corner of the passage leading to the nurses' home. She undressed quickly and got into bed, thinking of what he had said when they had parted. 'Max is one of my oldest friends, but I'll not interfere in his affairs, only—let him explain, Sophy.' The one thing she had no intention of doing, she decided, on a rising tide of anger.

She should have had a half day on Sunday, but Zuster Viske still had a sore throat. She could, she was told by authority, have an afternoon off and Casualty Sister would cover for her. There was no operating that morning; she busied herself, sometimes unnecessarily, doing little jobs that really didn't need doing, and went off duty as tired as though she had taken a heavy list. She hadn't eaten any breakfast; now she pecked at her dinner and went up to her room. Five minutes later she was curled up on her bed; it seemed a good idea to try and get some sleep. If it did nothing else, it might improve her looks, which, what with wakefulness and tears, were not at their best.

She had closed her eyes, and almost succeeded in banishing Max's white angry face from behind their lids, when there was a tentative tap at her door, and

Janie, looking enquiring and strangely apprehensive, poked her head round.

'Good. You are not sleeping—Dr Van Oosterwelde is downstairs. He says you are to go down and see him at once.'

Sophy propped her aching head on one elbow and said crossly, 'Tell him I won't.'

Janie's reaction to this forthright answer was immediate and severe. 'Sophy, you can't talk like that to a Prof: it's rude!'

Sophy thumped her pillow. 'Yes, it is, isn't it?' she agreed flatly. 'Would you rather I wrote it?'

But Janie was made of sterner stuff. 'No, indeed. I will tell him what you say.'

She was back within minutes. 'He says, if you do not go down, then he will come up.' She eyed Sophy uncertainly. 'He may not come up here—men may not come to your room.'

Sophy climbed off her bed. 'Very well, I'll come down.' She sounded meek, but there was nothing meek about the manner in which she jammed on her cap and tugged on her belt and cuffs, nor did she waste time on powder and lipstick, but kicked off her slippers, pushed her feet back into her neat black shoes, and pausing only to think Janie for her trouble, went downstairs.

Max was standing in the middle of the hall, watching her as she went down the stairs. She walked up to him, and focussed her eyes on a point below his chin.

'You wanted to see me, sir?'

'You know damn well I do.' He was quietly savage. 'You went away—I would have explained.'

She refocussed her eyes on his tie—Italian silk and a nice shade of blue. 'No need,' she said in a voice deliberately light, 'and if that is all... If you don't mind? I was taking a nap.'

He said very evenly. 'It is not all, and I do mind. You'll come back to Huys Oosterwelde with me— now. I want to talk to you.'

Despite her efforts, her voice rose. 'I'll not come, nor will I listen to you.'

Hans had come back into the hall from some errand or other. He was lingering outside his little office, near enough to hear them talking. Max glanced at him and said silkily,

'My dear good girl, if you don't walk down those steps and into the car, I swear I'll pick you up and carry you there.'

Sophy looked uncertain. 'You wouldn't dare...' She stole a look at him and decided that he would. Hans was watching them with an open interest, but she didn't think that his presence would make an iota of difference to Max's plans. She turned wordlessly, and walked beside him to the door and out into the courtyard; the cold wind made her shiver as it blew against her cotton dress.

He didn't speak on the way to Huys Oosterwelde. Only when they were in the hall and he was taking off his coat, he said over his shoulder, 'Take Miss Greenslade into the small sitting room, will you, Goeden?' He followed her in and said 'Sit down,' in the same curt voice, so that she immediately and naturally refused, standing very straight beside a circular walnut table. He shrugged his shoulders and went over to the fireplace and stood looking at her.

'Sophia, there is something I must tell you.'

She lifted her eyes briefly from the painstaking scrutiny she was giving the table. 'No. I have already told you that I don't want to hear. In any case, there's nothing to tell. I saw you—both of you—in the hall last night.'

Max watched her through narrowed lids. 'Yes? Go on.'

He strolled over to the french windows and let in Jack and Meg, who greeted him ecstatically before trotting over to the fire to spread themselves before its warmth. They had ignored Sophy, and Max said in a politely cool voice, 'I must apologise for my dogs' ill manners, Sophia.' He had gone back to the fireplace to lean against it, and stare at her.

Suddenly her rage and misery and humiliation boiled up and out in a torrent of words she didn't attempt to control.

'Don't dare call me Sophia to mock me! I hate you, and I hate myself for believing you last night and even more for forgetting poor Tineke—she was crying in your arms; breaking her heart, but how would you know that, for you have no heart. Oh, never mind me—I'm a nurse with no prospects and a plain face— fair game to such as you...' She was checked momentarily by the blazing anger in his white face, but her own anger spurred her on. 'But Tineke—how could you be so cruel? Why, you're nothing but a playboy; unscrupulous, and selfish and arrogant, safe behind your money and position and name...'

'Be quiet.' His voice was soft, but the chill of it froze her very bones. 'You've said enough, you don't need to labour the point. I cannot force you to listen to me, nor do I wish to do so.' He stirred Meg with a well-shod foot and went on in a quietly menacing voice, 'I should warn you that I cannot allow you to say these things.'

Sophy put a hand on the table and stood very straight in defiance of her trembling legs. 'I shall say what I like,' she said defiantly. She broke off as Goeden came in with a loaded tea tray which he put down on the table beside her and said, quiet-voiced,

'I expect Miss Greenslade would like a cup of tea before she goes back, sir—I took the liberty of bringing it in a little early.' He looked at Sophy in a fatherly way and murmured 'Cook thought you might like to try some of her muffins, miss.'

His master, however, did not share his solicitude for his guests' comfort. He waved a careless hand and said, 'Miss Greenslade won't require tea, Goeden, she will be returning immediately to hospital. Perhaps you will fetch the car—now.'

They stood in silence when he had gone, Max, his anger contained, relaxed, perfectly at ease. Sophy stood where she was, her anger gone, leaving her tired and listless; even in her low state of spirits able to appreciate the delicious smell coming from the muffin dish. There was bread and butter too, cut paper-thin, and tiny iced cakes. A cup of tea would be a great comfort. Her mouth watered; she had had no breakfast and only a pretence of dinner.

Max said suddenly from the fireplace, 'Are you hungry?'

'Yes,' said Sophy simply.

He looked at his watch, and said at his blandest, 'I'm sorry you are unable to stay for tea.' He stood looking at her, laughing softly, his handsome head on one side the better to study her discomfiture.

Sophy gulped. 'I hate you—do you hear?—hate you! I can think of nothing nicer than leaving Holland and never having to see you again!'

She took an urgent step backwards as he advanced towards her. It was of no use; he caught her by the shoulders with a grip that hurt and kissed her with slow deliberation, then let her go so suddenly that she had to clutch the table to keep on her feet. She put up a shaking hand and automatically straightened her cap, saying in a little voice, 'Oh, why did you do that?'

'My dear good girl—isn't that what you would expect from a playboy—an ageing playboy?' he added, on a bitter little laugh.

Sophy stared at his face. He didn't look like Max any more; although he was laughing she knew that he was angry still. Some of the things she had said seeped back into her mind; they had been awful—horrible. An urgent desire to take them all back was frustrated by the return of Goeden, who looked reproachfully at the tea tray before informing them that he had the car ready.

Sophy turned to go; she had wanted to say goodbye, but if she spoke now she would cry. Max had said nothing at all. She went through the door without looking back.

CHAPTER ELEVEN

THE MORNING'S LIST was a heavy one, and Sophy was glad of it. She welcomed the busy theatre routine as something familiar that she could depend upon. The first case was scheduled for eight-thirty, and came in promptly. Karel was anaesthetising; the change in his appearance was so marked that Sophy stared, wondering what could have happened to wipe away all trace of anxiety and worry from his face, but there was no time to talk, for Max, followed by Jan, had arrived promptly too. He wished her good morning, his eyes flickering over her as though she was someone he couldn't quite remember having met; they looked like blue ice. It was after eleven when he called a halt for coffee, and the three men went into the office followed by a nurse with the coffee tray, but Sophy stayed behind, ostensibly to put more blades in the Hibutane. When the nurse came back with a message that Professor van Oosterwelde wished her to take her coffee with him, she hesitated, unwilling to make an intolerable situation even more so. But on second thoughts she realised that Max was doing the only thing possible; they would have to work side by side for another week at least. On the surface they would have to continue on a friendly footing.

As she went into the tiny room, Max got up from the chair. 'Ah, Sister, there you are, do come and sit down.' He spoke pleasantly, but his eyes were chill as they met hers; she guessed his beautiful manners were hiding anger and even dislike. She shivered and took the mug of coffee Jan was holding out to her, and was for once thankful when he launched into an involved query about English public schools. She had just finished a painstaking explanation of higher education in England, when she became aware that Max was speaking.

'I have some good news for Sister,' he announced quietly, 'though I'm sure that you two are not likely to share her view. Zuster Smid telephoned me this morning—she is coming back this evening, to start work tomorrow. It seems ˜he does not want the holiday she was to have had after her quarantine.' He turned his head and looked at Sophy, sitting like a small whitefaced statue with wide, sad eyes, watching him. 'We shall be sorry to see you go, Sister Greenslade, although of course we are delighted to welcome Zuster Smid back again. You have been an excellent Theatre Sister, and we have all enjoyed working with you.'

He smiled at her, his eyes hard, and Sophy closed her own for a moment, then opened them quickly because Karel van Steen was speaking to her.

'You're very white, Sophy.' He looked at her kindly. 'Has the surprise been too much for you?'

Sophy achieved a smile. 'Yes, I think perhaps it was—but what a lovely one. I must see about my return home...'

Max cut in. 'That has all been arranged, Sister. You are booked on an afternoon flight tomorrow; naturally you want to go home as soon as possible.'

It seemed he couldn't get her out of the country fast enough. She heard Jan protesting, 'But, Professor, Sister might have stayed a few days on holiday.' He turned to Sophy. 'I'd love to show you something of Holland; you can't have seen much.'

Sophy smiled at him gratefully. 'That would have been very nice, and thank you for thinking of it, Jan, but I promised my family that I would go back just as soon as I wasn't needed here any more.' She hoped she had made the lie sound convincing. She stood up and went on with a gaiety she wasn't feeling, 'Well, all this excitement has made me quite light-headed. I think I'll go and check the instruments and get my mind back on my work.'

She smiled brilliantly at them all and went back to the theatre. She was far too seasoned a nurse to allow her private emotions to interfere with her job; she suppressed them sternly, and went about her work with her usual quiet competence. For once she was grateful for a curtailed lunch hour and the emergency appendix which had to be fitted in instead of a tea break. It was after six when they had finished and she took off the green gown for the last time and put it tidily in the bin. Max had disappeared, leaving the final stitching of the last case for Jan to do. He did it with his usual competence, then pulled off his gloves and wished her a regretful goodbye.

Karel, however, seemed disposed to linger. He looked at her curiously and asked, 'Are you really glad to be leaving us, Sophy?'

She said, too promptly, 'Oh, yes. It will be lovely to be home again.'

'Have you been so unhappy with us, then?'

Sophy arranged the cutting needles in meticulous order and said carefully, 'I've enjoyed my work here.'

He waited for her to continue, and when she didn't, asked, 'Has Max said goodbye to you yet?'

She remembered the disastrous conversation at Huys Oosterwelde, and said, 'No.'

Karel looked relieved. 'Oh, well. He will.'

Sophy thought that this was unlikely, but there seemed no point in saying so: she merely smiled and Karel went away, looking uncertain.

It was easier saying goodbye to the nurses in the ungrammatical mixture of English and Dutch words which had served them so well during her stay. The last one went away, and she was left in the theatre alone. Beyond saying goodbye to the Directrice and her personal farewells to some of the Sisters, she had finished at the hospital. She collected her cape and handbag and started off along the complex of corridors which would lead her to the nurses' home. It was a good thing that Max had gone; she wouldn't have known what to say to him. She rounded a corner, and there he was, talking to two of the surgical housemen. He looked up and watched her pass by, his face carved in granite. She no longer existed for him, she told herself fiercely; she was glad that she had said all the things she hadn't meant to say at all, but which had somehow tumbled out. She started to climb the stairs. Perhaps he would be happy again once she had gone. She stumbled a little, small and forlorn, and Max, who could see her from where he was standing, suddenly turned his back on the sight of her and strode away, leaving two astonished young men in mid-sentence.

*　　*　　*

Sophy sat in her room the next morning, doing nothing. She had said goodbye to the Directrice, who had been charming; and to the Sisters whom she had grown to like so much, and now, because she had got up very early to finish her packing, she had nothing more to occupy her. At five o'clock, unable to sleep, it had seemed a sensible idea to occupy herself with the numerous little jobs which would make day seem nearer, but now she saw her mistake. She looked at her watch: it was barely midday. The taxi—for Max had arranged for a taxi too—would fetch her at half-past three. She could go out, she supposed, and decided against it, refusing to admit to herself that she wanted to stay under the same roof as Max until the last minute. There seemed little point in going to lunch; she sat on her bed, contemplating her shoes, her thoughts jostling each other around her tired brain.

When somebody knocked on the door, she called 'Come in' without looking up. The maid for the bed linen, probably.

It was Tineke van der Wijde. Sophy got off the bed, but before she could speak, Tineke said, 'Sophy, I had to see you—Karel telephoned me. It's a surprise, your leaving like this. I mean, I thought you would be here for another week.'

Sophy, white-faced, pulled forward the little easy chair by the window. 'Please sit down. I'm glad you've come. I—I wanted to see you, but I didn't think that you would want to see me, so I wrote you a letter; I was going to post it at Schiphol.' She watched Tineke unfasten her fur coat and sit down. She looked radiant—probably she had seen Max…

'I want to tell you how sorry I am,' began Sophy, 'about last night. I'm so ashamed. You see, I like you; I wouldn't hurt you for the world, and I did. When I saw you and Max in the hall afterwards I felt so small and mean—could you forget about it? You see, it doesn't matter—Max was only—he didn't mean anything, you know.' She stopped a minute to steady her voice. 'I'll be gone in an hour or two, and you'll forget me, and I know Max will be glad that I've gone.'

Tineke sat forward in her chair. 'You love Max, don't you, Sophy?'

Sophy looked up briefly. 'Yes. But I shall get over it.'

'Karel says that you and Max have quarrelled—oh, Max said nothing, but Karel could see... Did Max talk to you last night?'

'No, I left early.'

'Because you saw me and Max in the hall, and I was in his arms?'

'Yes.'

Tineke got up and walked over to the bed, where she made herself comfortable beside Sophy. 'Now, listen to me,' she said. 'There is a great deal you should know. I have been a fool; I should have told you right at the beginning, for Max would not, for it is not his secret, but mine—mine and Karel's.

'Until last night, Karel had a wife—hopelessly insane for nine years. He and I—we have loved each other for many years. I will not tell you all now, there is no time—but we were young together. When my husband died, I came back to Holland, and Karel and I knew that we had not changed. But Karel was a doctor with a fine career and he was a Roman Catholic too—so you see, there could be no divorce. Max knew about us; he has been our friend since we were at school together. He saw that we could not go on as we were—meeting by chance at some dance or party, never to be alone together, so one day he said to me, "Tineke, you and I are going to become very close friends, so that in a little while everyone will think that one day we shall marry. We shall go everywhere together and you shall spend each weekend at my home, and I promise you that Karel shall be there too, and no one will need to know." Dear Max! So many dances he has taken me to, so that I might dance just once with Karel, and so many dull evenings at Huys Oosterwelde, sitting in his study, so that Karel and I could be alone together. We went to the nursing home last night—Max and Karel and I— and Max went back before us because he said he had to talk to you, but of course, you were not there. But now everything is all right, for you know now that Max and I do not love each other at all, and you will have time to see him now, and explain.'

She got up and fastened her coat and bent and kissed Sophy on the cheek. 'I am so happy,' she said, 'I want you to be happy too. You are so right for Max.' She smiled. 'And now Karel and I can marry.'

When she had gone, Sophy went back to the bed and sat down again. If she hadn't behaved so badly towards Max she could have gone and found him. As it was, she would have to sit where she was, waiting for the taxi to take her on the first stage of her journey home. She hadn't realised until that moment that Max had deliberately called Zuster Smid back so that he could send her home as soon as possible. Two tears rolled down her cheeks, and she wiped them away angrily. She had only herself to thank, nothing had been altered. There was something she could do, though, something she owed Max. She rummaged round in her luggage and found her writing case, opened it, then went and sat at the little table by the window, but the right words wouldn't come; after a long while, she looked at her watch and saw that it was three o'clock. She put it away again and fastened her baggage, dressed herself in her thick tweed coat and the little fur hat and went downstairs to the front hall, where she found Hans. She asked him to send a porter for her bags and take them out to the taxi when it arrived, and ask the driver to go round to the side exit from Out-Patients. She wished Hans goodbye, and then, before she could change her mind, started down the passage leading to Out-Patients.

There weren't many people in the waiting room; two elderly ladies having a cosy gossip about their insides, an old man reading a newspaper and eating a roll out of a bag, and a young frightened girl. Sophy made her way over to the little desk in the corner, smiling at the girl as she passed her, for she looked lonely. The nurse on duty was one Sophy knew slightly. She looked up and said in surprise, 'I thought you had gone, Zuster Greenslade.' She spoke in Dutch, and Sophy who had tried very hard with the language, said '*Nog niet, Zuster*,' with a vile accent, and tried to think of some more Dutch words, but there was no time to waste, so she said in English,

'May I see Professor van Oosterwelde, please?'

The nurse understood. 'I tell him,' she said cheerfully, and got up.

Sophy said 'No!' so sharply that the nurse looked at her in astonishment. It was fortunate that a patient came out of the surgery at that moment. Sophy went to the door, regardless of the indignant voice of one of the gossiping ladies who was next. 'Five minutes,' she said imploringly over her shoulder, and went in.

Max was sitting at his desk, writing up notes; he didn't look up but said in Dutch, 'Come in and sit down, please.' After a minute he pushed the papers away and saw who it was. Sophy watched his face empty itself of all expression, so that it wasn't Max at all, but a polite, bland mask. She glanced at the clock on the wall; the second hand had already swept away one of her precious minutes. Max looked at the clock too and said, with a cold courtesy belied by the blaze of anger in his eyes,

'This is unexpected; I regret that I am unable to see you...' He waved a hand at the pile of notes on the desk. 'Your taxi will be waiting, should you not go? You don't want to miss your plane.'

'I don't care,' said Sophy. 'There's something I must say to you before I leave.'

The mask cracked into a mocking smile. 'Something else? I can assure you that you overlooked nothing in the catalogue of my sins and vices.' He picked up his pen. 'Miss Greenslade, you and I have nothing more to say to each other.' There was finality in his voice; he drew some papers towards him and started to write.

Painful colour crept into Sophy's white face. She paused long enough to choke back the sobs crowding into her throat, and said doggedly, 'Please listen; I'm sorry I said those dreadful things to you on Sunday. None of them was true—at least, you are arrogant sometimes, but only when you want your own way—'

Max had put down his pen and was sitting back in his chair, looking down so that she could not see his face; the small sound which escaped his lips was, she supposed, one of disgust.

She sniffed inelegantly to hold back the tears which, Luke had been at pains to tell her from their earliest quarrels, were unsporting. Her pleasant voice was rigidly controlled as she went on, 'I apologise for calling you a playboy and for vilifying your good name. I suppose if I had been a man, you would have knocked me down...'

Max lifted his head and looked at her searchingly through narrowed lids. 'Er—yes, I imagine I should have done so. I had to be content with denying you your tea.'

He sounded as though he was laughing. It made it very difficult, but she had to finish, now she had started, and time was running out. 'I'm not making excuses, they wouldn't make any difference, would they? You'll not forgive me, and I don't blame you, but I must tell you the truth before I go. I...owe it to you. I lied when I told you that I hated you. I've always loved you, Max, since we met, and I still do...'

There was the sound of a chair scraping along the floor outside; the next patient was on her way. Sophy said in quiet despair, 'Goodbye, Max,' and slipped past the woman who had opened the door behind her. The nurse was talking to the old man; they both looked up as Sophy went blindly past them and out through the door into the corridor. There was no one to see her turn down the bleak door-lined passage leading to the side entrance. She hurried down it, taking small sobbing breaths, not bothering to mop her streaming eyes—she could do that presently in the taxi.

She was level with the last door when it was opened without haste and an arm, immaculate in its finely tailored cloth, shot out and Max's large hand clamped down on her shoulder, bringing her to a sudden awkward halt. She stood looking up at him through a blur of tears, and then, because she couldn't see him clearly; angrily dashed a hand across her eyes, leaving a wet, faintly grubby smear. Her ordinary face looked quite plain, and any dignity she might have had left was dispelled by the prodigious sniff she gave.

'Go away,' said Sophy, and gave an experimental wriggle.

The grip on her shoulder tightened. Max said softly, 'Shall we finish our conversation? If I remember, it was becoming most interesting when you saw fit to leave.'

She found her voice. 'Please let me go—you said we hadn't any more to say to each other.' She added desperately, 'I shall miss my plane.'

'So you will.' He pulled her, not gently, into the room. It was used for board meetings, or some such thing, and had a long heavy table at its centre and chairs arranged stiffly against the walls. Sophy retreated until she felt the hard rim of the table at her back, and watched fascinated as Max shut and locked the door, then took the key out and strode over to the table and laid it on the table, close to her.

'You can open the door and go when you want to,' he said equably. He picked up her hands in turn and drew off her gloves, then unbuttoned her coat. Sophy hardly noticed what he was doing and when she did, her protest died on her lips under his level gaze. It was Professor Jonkheer Maximillan van Oosterwelde standing in front of her—not Max. He addressed her now in a cool professional voice.

'Why did you wait until you were leaving?' he asked.

Sophy didn't pretend to misunderstand him. 'I didn't—not deliberately. Tineke came to see me this afternoon. I tried to write to you afterwards, but it wouldn't...I couldn't...' She paused. 'So I came to see you, otherwise I should have been a coward. I know you won't believe me ever again, but you must see that I had to tell you.' She started to button up her coat. 'I'm going now, whatever you say.' Her throat ached with the effort to speak in a normal voice.

She didn't look at him, although she longed most desperately to do so, but when he said, 'Look at me, Sophia,' in a compelling tone, she raised her head to meet his gaze and was breathless at its enchantment.

'It wasn't my secret to tell, Sophia,' he said. He had made no effort to touch her, yet it was as though his arms were already around her. 'Not until last night—and you had gone.' He smiled at her and Sophy felt her heart leap at the tenderness of it. He took her hand, still clutching at a coat button, and said on a laugh, 'Do you suppose I can propose to you in five minutes, for that is all the time I have, my darling.'

He walked over to the telephone in the far corner of the room, and Sophy listened while he told the nurse crisply that he was delayed for five minutes, and then he got through to Hans and instructed him about the taxi and her luggage. He was still smiling as he came back to her, and this time his arms really were around her; they felt like all the love and security and comfort that the world could hold. She stood in the magic circle he had created for her, and when he kissed her with a fierce tenderness that took her breath she knew that her dreams of happiness were no longer dreams but reality. When he let her go, she whispered, 'Max—oh, Max,' and smiled her beautiful smile so that he kissed her again, gently this time.

'Sophia, I love you—have loved you since the moment I first saw you coming down the road towards me.' His blue eyes were very bright, searching hers. 'Marry me, my dearest girl. We'll go to England— it's quicker there, and we've wasted so much time already.'

Sophy stood on tip-toe and kissed him. 'I'll marry you as soon as you like, Max,' she hesitated, 'darling,' she said shyly, and was kissed breathless for her pains.

'Will you wait here, sweetheart? I shall be fifteen— perhaps twenty minutes.'

He cupped her face in his hands, so that she could see deep into his eyes and know for always how much he loved her. After a long moment he straightened up and walked quickly away and through the door at the far end of the room, leaving her to stand and dream. She was aroused from this delightful occupation by a tap on the door. The key was still on the table; she picked it up, wondering who it could be. It was Hans, looking like a conspiratorial uncle and bearing a tea tray.

'Professor van Oosterwelde telephoned that I was to bring you an English tea.'

He smiled at her all over his kind face, put the tray on the table, accepted her thanks with dignity and disappeared. Sophy realised all at once that tea and toast were the two things she most longed for—breakfast had been hours ago; she'd had no lunch. She drank the tea and consumed the toast—somehow Max's thoughtfulness augured well for their future. Much refreshed, she went to work on her face, managing as best she might with the tiny mirror in her bag. She had taken the pins out of her mousy tresses and was combing them smooth when Max came back into the room, wearing a top coat and carrying a bulky briefcase. He put the case on the table and went and stood close to her. 'I have often wondered what your hair would look like hanging down your back—the temptation to remove the pins was sometimes very great.'

Sophy was twisting the thick coil neatly, pushing in pins with lightning precision. 'I meant to be ready for you, Max, but the tea was so delicious. Thank you for thinking about it.'

He had gone over to the chair where her coat was. 'I shall spend the rest of my life thinking of things to make you happy, my dearest.'

They smiled at each other across the room. 'So shall I, dear Max.'

She stood up. 'Max? I don't even know where I'm going…'

He helped her into her coat and turned her round to face him and started to do up the buttons. 'You're going home, darling, to Huys Oosterwelde. Grandmother will play propriety for us until I can arrange for us to go to England.'

They walked through the hospital, to the front door, where Hans appeared like a benevolent genie and wished them a sly good evening. It had just turned four o'clock and the afternoon was darkening, the sky crowded with heavy clouds sailing ponderously before a biting wind. Max walked Sophy briskly to the Rolls, and when she got in, leaned down and kissed her, his mouth hard against hers, before he shut the door.

The roads were almost empty; it was hardly the day for a pleasure drive, and it was still too early for the hordes of home-going cars. Max drove slowly along the road by the river. The water looked like pale steel under the lowering sky, the houses bordering it remote against their wintry background, their carefully-tended trees blowing to and fro and the water breaking into uneasy ripples before the wind. The short journey seemed even shorter by reason of the amount they had to say to each other, but when they reached the tall wrought iron gates, they fell silent as Max turned the car into the short drive. Huys Oosterwelde lay before them; its grey stone merging into the greyness of the day. Its windows glowed with light—they could see Goeden waiting for them, standing in the radiance streaming from the open door. Max stopped.

'Home, sweetheart,' he said, and put an arm around Sophy. They sat in silence, sharing happiness. Presently she stirred against his shoulder.

'Who built this house, Max?'

He quoted. 'Maximillan, born 1569, married Juliana…'

'And loved her dearly,' added Sophy. 'How many children did they have?'

She felt his hold tighten.

'Five—no, six. Three of each.'

'I hope history repeats itself,' said Sophy.

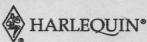

REGENCY
ROMANCE

Transport yourself to the grace and charm
of an era gone by...where opulence is the
rule and captivating adventures between
feisty heroines and roguish heroes
entertain with enchanting wit.

*Experience the enchanting world of Regency romance
in November 2001 with these four titles:*

THE SILVER SQUIRE
by Mary Brendan

A BARGAIN WITH FATE
by Ann Elizabeth Cree

LADY KNIGHTLEY'S
SECRET
by Anne Ashley

THE ADMIRAL'S
DAUGHTER
by Francesca Shaw

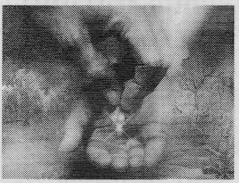